The Merriman Chronicles

Book Four

The Threat in the East

Copyright Information

The Merriman Chronicles - Book 4

The Threat In The East

Copyright © 2014 by Roger Burnage

With the exception of certain well known historical figures, the characters in this book have no relation or resemblance to any person living or dead.

All rights reserved. This book and all "The Merriman Chronicles" are works of fiction. No part of this book may be reproduced or used in any manner without written permission of the copyright owner except for the use of quotations in a book review.

Sixth Edition – 2024

Updated by: Robin Burnage
Edited by: Katharine D'Souza

ISBN: 9798343175042 (Paperback)
ISBN: 9798343175684 (Hardcover)

www.merriman-chronicles.com

Books in the series

James Abel Merriman (1768 – 1843)

A Certain Threat
The Threat in the West Indies
Merriman and the French Invasion
The Threat in the East
The Threat in the Baltic
The Threat in the Americas
The Threat in the Adriatic
The Threat in the Atlantic

Edward James Merriman (1853 - 1928)

The Fateful Voyage

Foreword

Author's notes

In the spring of 1998, workmen demolishing an old nursing home in the country to the north-west of Chester, discovered bundles of old papers concealed behind a bricked up fireplace. One of the men with more perspicacity than his fellows rescued the papers from the bonfires of rubbish and gave them to his employer, a builder, who, knowing of my interest in such things passed them on to me. The discovered papers were mostly in a very bad state due to the effects of dampness, mildew and the depredations of vermin over the years, and many of the oldest bundles were totally illegible. Another obvious problem was that the papers had been written by different people and some of the handwriting was not of the best. Sorting the papers into chronological order took many months of part time effort, indeed I gave up on the job for weeks and months at a time, but as I progressed with the work I realised that it was a history of the Merriman family from the late 18th century to the early years of the 20th century.

The first clearly decipherable writings referred to a certain James Abel Merriman, a naval officer at the time of the Napoleonic wars, and revealed some startling facts about French activities in and around Ireland and the Irish Sea at that time. I quickly realised that I had in my hands the material for a novel or *novels about a little known part of our history. Other papers showed that beside those serving in the navy, other members of the family were connected with the 22nd Regiment of Foot, the Cheshire Regiment. Intriguingly, a family tree was among the papers in one of the later bundles. Armed with that and from research in local archives, church records etc., it appeared that the last direct male heir of the family, Albert George Merriman was killed in France in 1916 and the last descendant, his unmarried sister Amy Elizabeth, a nurse, was also killed in France in 1917.*

I have written several novels about members of the Merriman family whose members served their country and sometimes died for it and I have collected them under the heading "The Merriman Chronicles".

Roger Burnage.

Chapter One

The Threat - Napoleon

The year 1798

His Majesty's frigate Lord Stevenage heeled sharply as a particularly savage gust of wind hit her. Foul weather had troubled her for the last few days and all aboard hoped that conditions would improve. The wind had slackened and occasional glimpses of sun had appeared through gaps in the racing clouds. If there was one person aboard who really longed for the ship's pitching and rolling to cease it was Mr Grahame. He had never been a good sailor and had fled below to take refuge in his cabin as soon as the ship encountered the first heavy seas.

Captain James Merriman grinned as he saw this. Grahame was one of many agents of the Treasury which at that time coordinated all of Britain's espionage services under the Prime Minister, William Pitt, and Lord Stevenage. He was one of the most experienced and capable agents and over the last few months he and Merriman had been responsible for the capture of a French agent in Ireland and the recovery of several important documents detailing French activities, spies and collaborators in Portugal, the Eastern Mediterranean, and even India.

During that adventure, Merriman and his ship the *Lord Stevenage* had captured a French corvette, a small frigate really, and also a merchant ship, *The Fat Frog,* so called by a witty crewman because they couldn't pronounce the French name. Both ships had been bought in by the Admiralty and Merriman had deposited his share of the prize money into his account with the agent in Portsmouth. Of course the crews were happy to get their share too, small though it was.

Merriman and Grahame had gone to London to report to the Admiralty where they met with the same Admiral Sir David

Edwards as the last time they were there. Also at the meeting was Grahame's spymaster, Lord Stevenage. Both men were in deep conversation when Merriman and Grahame were ushered in but broke off to welcome them. After the usual civilities had been exchanged, they all took their places around the imposing mahogany table that Merriman remembered from his previous visits.

The Admiral said, "Captain Merriman, I must congratulate you again on the success of your last foray into Ireland and the capture of the French agent Moreau. That was well done but now I must give you some bad news. Before you left for Ireland, rumour had it that Napoleon was putting a fleet together to take an army to Egypt from where he might be able to threaten and perhaps even attack India to join with Tipu Sahib, the ruler of Mysore. As you will know, he is a firm ally of the French and no friend of ours. A British fleet under Admiral Nelson is hoping to intercept him but we don't know yet what has happened. Perhaps Mr Grahame could advise you further."

"Indeed I can, sir," Grahame replied. "As you know, James, all countries have spies and agents in opposing countries and we have ours in France, indeed in Paris itself. I am commanded by the Prime Minister himself to go to India to find out what I can of French activity there. It is not a rumour, our people have confirmed it. Napoleon intends to attack Egypt. He proposed the campaign to the ruling Directory last year, telling them that he intended to undermine Britain's access to India to fulfil his dream of linking up with Tipu Sahib and his large, French-trained army. The Directory approved it and since then he has been gathering a large army and fleet in Toulon intending to sail as soon as possible."

"I see," said Merriman.

"After defeating Egypt, although he won't find that easy because the Mamelukes are fierce warriors, Napoleon intends to march south and collect another fleet to take the army down the Red Sea and across to India. All this is true, gentlemen, our best agents in France, all reliable people, have confirmed it." Grahame paused to take a sip of water then continued, "We also know for a fact that Tipu intends to build a navy. His father had a few ships, mainly used to protect his merchant fleet, but Tipu is aiming to build a fleet of some forty warships of seventy two and sixty two cannon. If he succeeds he will have the biggest and most powerful navy in Asia." He paused and shook his head. "But we have had no more recent news from our people in India."

Merriman took a few moments to absorb all that and consider the ramifications of Napoleon's plans. "This is terrible news, gentlemen. If Napoleon succeeds, he and this Tipu man would be able to isolate India and force us out."

"Yes, that is certain to happen unless he can be stopped, James," said Lord Stevenage, who had been silent until then, merely nodding to confirm what had been said. "I am sure that you can see what you will be called upon to do. You are to take Mr Grahame to Bombay where he will endeavour to find out for us how far Tipu's naval building has progressed. The East India Company has requested the navy's help to protect their shipping from pirates. I say pirates but some of them could be some of Tipu's own ships. That will be your main duty and also to support Mr Grahame as you have done so well in the Past"

The Admiral nodded. "That is it, Captain. Your ship will be stored and supplied for an extended voyage and you will return to Portsmouth and put to sea immediately your ship is ready. The dockyard has been told to expedite the work. I trust you will have a speedy voyage and that you both meet with success."

They had returned to the ship carrying with them their written orders. Merriman's were to take Grahame to Lisbon and then Gibraltar from whence he could send the information about French spies and their collaborators aboard a King's ship to Naples and Greece. It would then go to Britain's man in the consulate who coordinated the English agents in that part of the world. From Gibraltar, their orders sent Merriman and Grahame on to India.

While Merriman had been absent in London, back in Portsmouth, Acting Fourth Lieutenant Alfred Shrigley had passed his examination meaning he was now a fully qualified officer. He had managed to stay with the *Lord Stevenage* thanks to the Port Admiral Sir George FitzHerbert who had been earnestly requested by Merriman to allow Shrigley to stay. Mr Laing, the First Lieutenant, had managed to find seven more men to replace those lost previously. An uninspiring lot, jailbirds all who had chosen service in the navy instead of deportation or hanging.

A new young midshipman had also joined the ship in Portsmouth. He was only twelve years old, one Edward Green, who at first was terribly sea sick but fought his stomach valiantly and very quickly adjusted to life aboard. Merriman had interviewed him when he joined the ship and found him to be intelligent and wanting to learn. With his red hair and blue eyes he reminded Merriman of Alan Jones, his former First Lieutenant and friend aboard his first command, the brig *Conflict*. Jones had been killed during a fight with corsairs off Africa. Green would be the most junior, below the other two midshipmen, Alan Hungerford, sixteen and now the ship's signals officer, and Gideon Small who had only just turned thirteen.

They found Lisbon to be a pleasant city, much of it being rebuilt after the recent earthquakes had demolished many buildings. The temperature was like the Mediterranean at that time of year, very pleasant after the cold and stormy passage from England. Merriman watched as the ship passed the famous Belem Tower, built in the 16th century by King Manuel 1st as part of the fortifications at the mouth of the Tagus to safeguard the people of Lisbon from attack from the sea.

The *Lord Stevenage* anchored near the bustling harbour and, after the usual formalities with the Portuguese officials, Mr Grahame hurried off to find the British Consulate. There he would pass on the new information about the activities of French agents in Spain and Portugal to England's main agent.

After ensuring that water and fresh fruit could be supplied, Merriman left the arrangements in the hands of his second officer and Grummage the purser whilst he sat at his desk to write letters home to his family and to his new wife, Helen.

Almost daily during the past weeks, Merriman had thought about what his new wife Helen would be doing and, not for the first time, he recalled the passionate few days they had spent together shortly before Admiralty orders took him away. *Have I had left her with child? If I have, I will know nothing about it, except maybe by post, until I return home again, months or perhaps years ahead. And my parents too. Mother was gravely ill when I left. She was being looked after by Helen's father, William Simpson, who is an excellent doctor. He kept her alive to see her son's wedding but I do not expect to see her again. And Father, now an old man, would he live long after his wife's death?* Merriman shook his head, there was no time now for such thoughts. There was much else to be done.

Gibraltar was the next port of call and, as they passed Spain, now allied to the French, a wary lookout was kept in case any Spanish warships put in an appearance. None did and the straits of Gibraltar gave them no problems. Once anchored in the harbour under the looming bulk of the great Rock, Merriman and Grahame reported to the Admiral in the naval headquarters. They requested him to arrange for Grahame's dispatches to go in a King's ship bound for Italy and Greece to deliver the new information about French agents in the Eastern Mediterranean. Grahame's documents ensured the Admiral's co-operation.

Merriman seized the opportunity to have any ship's mail put ashore for eventual delivery to England. He had been writing letters to his parents and Helen, adding a paragraph or two every day, but when they would be delivered was anybody's guess.

During the last months and years Merriman and Grahame had worked together so frequently that they had become good friends. Merriman was pleased by what Grahame had said to him before they left Gibraltar. "I have enjoyed working with you, James. We seem to think alike and our last adventures have both proved to be more successful than we could have hoped. Let us hope that our next venture in India will be equally successful."

"Yes, sir, let us hope so. It has been a long time since I was there."

Briefly Merriman's mind drifted back to the days in the Indian Ocean when he served as a Lieutenant aboard the frigate *Calcutta* and to memories of the action in which they had captured a French brig renamed *Conflict* which he had been ordered to take back to Gibraltar with dispatches. Hastily returning his thoughts to the present, he hurried back on deck to confirm that the replenishment of fresh water had been completed and to issue the orders needed to set sail for the long journey ahead.

Chapter Two

En route to India

Once under way and all sight of Gibraltar was lost astern, Merriman called his officers down to his cabin to inform them of the Admiralty orders. The Master, Mr Cuthbert, was first to arrive. He was an elderly man, grey-haired and with a weather-beaten face, legacy of his years at sea. He had a pronounced stoop due to having to bend low to avoid striking his head on the beams above him. Merriman noticed that he still favoured his side where he had received a severe splinter wound over four years ago. He was followed in by Lieutenant Andrews and the other officers together with the marine officers. Young Green stood in a corner with his mouth open, obviously overwhelmed at being in the presence of so many of his seniors. The other young Midshipman, Gideon Small, was used to it and Merriman had noticed that the two youngsters were becoming fast friends.

Merriman looked round at his men for a few moments before speaking. "Sit down, gentlemen, I have news for you."

Mr Cuthbert immediately took the best chair, claiming the privilege due to his age, whilst the others sat on the few chairs and benches.

When all were settled, Merriman began. "I have no doubt it will come as no surprise to you that we are bound for India."

There was a stir of excitement at the news but Merriman quickly called for order.

"I want you, Mr Cuthbert, to set the best course for the Cape of South Africa as the winds allow."

Mr Cuthbert replied, "Aye-aye, sir. I've done that voyage often enough. I have all the charts I need. May I ask, sir, to which coast of India are we going?"

"Indeed you may. It will be the Malabar coast as we have to go to Bombay first to speak with the Governor and the senior members of the Honourable East India Company there. They are having trouble with French privateers and Arab pirates to the extent that they dare not send many merchant ships back to England unless in convoy, although the biggest Indiamen are quite well armed and can usually take care of themselves. The Company's small naval force, the Bombay Marine, is quite unable to cope with the problem and the Admiralty has ordered us to reinforce the Marine and to try and seek out and destroy as many of these cutthroats as we can. Now, Mr Grahame, perhaps you would explain to these gentlemen what you know about Napoleon's plans for Egypt and India?"

As Grahame recited what was known, the faces of the officers registered shock and amazement and then the usually calm officers plied Merriman with questions. He laughingly answered, "I'm sorry, gentlemen, I know little more than we have told you. We will have to wait until we reach Bombay. Mr Andrews, doubtless we will need our fair weather sails, so have them checked over again. The bos'n tells me that they should be all right but remember that we have never used them since commissioning and, after the soaking the ship received in the Irish Sea, I don't want any trouble with them. So have them brought up and aired. We should have plenty of sun soon which will help."

Andrews nodded.

"Mr McBride, I trust you have all you need to look after the men."

"Indeed I have, sir. You will remember that your father-in-law, the good Doctor Simpson, gave me much knowledge of the health problems in the tropics before we went to the West Indies."

"Doctor Simpson was employed by the East India Company for many years before retiring home to England," Merriman explained to the others. "Thank you, Mr McBride. I will arrange to call at as many ports as possible to buy fresh vegetables and citrus fruit to stop the spread of scurvy as you know it does."

Gideon Small, the little Midshipman, put his hand in the air and asked, "How does it stop scurvy, sir?"

"That is a very good question, Mr Small. I can't tell you all the medical details but you can ask the Doctor afterwards. I do know that a Scottish doctor, in the navy, discovered this many years ago and the Admiralty have only recently woken up to his work and issued orders that citrus fruit should be obtained whenever possible. Right, gentlemen, I think that is all for now."

The officers filed out and Merriman noticed that Small followed the Doctor closely. A good lad that one, not afraid of asking questions. I think he will make a good officer in time.

The voyage southwards continued and, as they passed the coast of Morocco and north Africa to port, Merriman found himself recalling the events in those waters more than four years ago. The wild fight with the two corsair ships to save an Indiaman and passengers, the loss of his ship, the brig *Conflict,* and the fortunate meeting with Lord Stevenage on the Indiaman. That meeting had been very eventful as it eventually transpired that Merriman's father and Lord Stevenage were cousins. Stevenage had been instrumental in obtaining Merriman's last command, the sloop *Aphrodite,* and his present command, the frigate *Lord Stevenage,* which Merriman had named after his lordship.

Chapter Three

The Indian Ocean

The *Lord Stevenage* was now well on her way and taking every advantage of the favourable wind to push her northward up the Indian Ocean. The erratic and fickle winds that had plagued the ship over the last months had, once they rounded the southern tip of Africa, settled at last to a reasonably steady wind and the ship was making good progress. On the whole, Merriman was happy with the ship's officers and crew except for two of the seven new men. Five of them had soon, though resentfully, learned their duties, spread out among the seasoned hands but, in the Boatswain's words, the other two, Smithers and Greely, were, "Bloody useless bastards. Troublemakers from the start and violent with it."

In general, the crew was well trained and willing, gunnery was excellent and the whole ship was in good order. Merriman reminded himself not to be too complacent. He must watch for anything which might affect his ship's performance. Once in the Indian Ocean, there would be fighting to do so the guns must be regularly exercised to maintain the standard he required.

He knew he could rely on his officers to watch everything as well. Jack was usually too busy to think about anything else but Merriman knew that, should the ship become becalmed in the tropics for long, the heat from the scorching sun blazing down from a cloudless sky would be enough to cause grumbling and worse, even with shade awnings spread. The biggest problem would be boredom. Apart from all the work needed daily for the ship's maintenance, the task of keeping the crew happy all that time was essential.

In the past, Merriman had organised competitions of various kinds, fishing for example, races up the rigging, swimming when the ship was becalmed with a keen watch kept for sharks. Sometimes they even had entertainment by those men who could sing or play a musical instrument. Even the foolish tricks that the simple minded Biggins played on members of the crew were tolerated by them. Indeed they treated him as something of a mascot and helped him with his simple duties to ensure that he did not fall foul of authority. All assumed that the livid scar on the side of his head, received in some fight with the French, whom he hated, probably explained his mental difficulties.

Of course Merriman and Grahame spent many hours together, discussing what might happen when they reached Bombay.

"We have two agents there, James, but we have heard nothing from them for at least a twelvemonth and so I must find out if they are still alive," mused Grahame, his voice serious.

"You have been deep in thought since we left Gibraltar, sir," said Merriman on one occasion. "Is there something particular I should know about?"

"Yes, James, there is, and I will tell you all about it when I have thought out the various possibilities involved."

The biggest cause for amusement during the journey was meeting King Neptune, when all seamen and marines who had not crossed the equator were subjected to inquisition and punishment by Neptune. The Master, Mr Cuthbert, was dressed as King Neptune with a long wig and beard made out of rope strands. He carried a fearsome looking trident. His 'court' consisted of some of the ship's warrant officers rigged out with wigs and beards and some kind of fancy dress. The uninitiated were confined below then brought up on deck one by one to meet Neptune and his 'court' who decided what his initiation punishment would be. Usually this was to be smeared in tallow or grease before being pushed into the belly of a sail rigged on deck and filled with seawater. The man's gleeful mates kept on dunking him until Neptune told them to stop.

Even Mr Grahame laughingly submitted to the indignity, though the two troublemakers, Greely and Smithers, fought tooth and nail to avoid their fate. Their struggles were to no avail as they were each roughly dragged forward, smeared with more tallow and dunked repeatedly and for longer than the rest.

Watching from the quarterdeck rail, Merriman knew that a careful watch would have to be kept on both of them.

Later he called all the officers and petty officers to his cabin and stressed the need to keep an eye on the two problematic new men. "We could have real difficulty with them, gentlemen. As Shakespeare says, I think in Julius Caesar, 'Yon Cassius hath a lean and hungry look and such men are dangerous.' There is no knowing what they may get up to after this."

Merriman did not know how right he was.

Chapter Four

The first Pirate victim

In the event the voyage to India passed reasonably quickly. Merriman spent a lot of time with his officers, playing cards, reading books and even Shakespeare's plays. Mr Grahame taught him chess and the third Lieutenant and the new midshipman Green proved to be fairly proficient so that many hours passed in that way. Every day Merriman added another paragraph or two to a letter to his wife, though he had no idea when he could send it on a ship bound for England. Even gunnery time improved due to the competition between larboard and starboard watches and the races by the Topmen to be the first to the masthead. The races by the Waisters, men who had no skill aloft, from stem to stern of the ship were popular, keeping all the men fit because nobody was spared except for the surgeon and old Mr Cuthbert, the Master. Merriman even insisted that he and all the officers took part. So he had a contented and fit crew for whatever lay ahead. The midshipmen were beginning to show proficiency in navigation under the careful instructions of Mr Cuthbert.

Captain St James, the senior marine officer, an excellent and very proficient swordsman, continued to practice with Merriman and the other officers. Indeed Merriman had been a reasonably good swordsman and the regular practice had certainly improved his abilities. With that and some of the tricks not approved of by fencing tutors but taught to him by St James, he felt more than capable of holding his own.

And so the voyage had continued. Merriman had known it could take four or even five months to reach India from England. Long before then the drinking water would have developed a scum on it with slime on the inside of the barrels and the biscuits would be like iron and full of maggots. The salt meat in casks should still be edible, although there would almost certainly be some casks of rotten meat mixed in by money grabbing, conniving naval contractors. Happily, they had been able to find fresh water and food at Gibraltar and the Cape Verde Islands and then later at Simonstown in South Africa which had recently been captured from the Dutch at the battle of Muizenberg with few casualties on either side.

The ship was now heading north northeast in the Indian Ocean, well offshore to avoid the southward Agulhas current and to catch the monsoon winds blowing northward towards India. They kept well to the east of Madagascar and the Seychelles and were nearly at the latitude of the southern tip of India which was just out of sight on the starboard side. Merriman was beginning to congratulate himself on a good voyage when one day in the forenoon a hail from the sailor on watch aloft on the foremast brought him up on deck. The officer of the watch, Lieutenant Weston, quickly reported to him.

"Something right ahead, sir, but it can't be properly identified. I've sent Larkin aloft with a telescope to see if he can make anything of it."

The Lieutenant had hardly finished speaking when there came a hail from Larkin, who had the sharpest eyes aboard. "Deck there, it looks like a ship upside down, sir, barely awash but there is somebody lying on the keel, sir."

"Keep well to windward of it, Mr Weston," ordered Merriman. "And when we are level, heave to and I'll have an armed boat ready for lowering. These seas are infested with pirates and privateers so we'll take no chances."

When the ship was lying hove to, the wreck could be seen clearly. A wreck it was, with the keel almost all that could be seen and a man or boy lying on it who feebly waved when the boat approached. He was lucky, sharks were circling the wreck and hardly had he been dragged aboard when the last part of the keel slipped down out of sight. The survivor proved to be no more than a boy, dreadfully burned by the sun, now unconscious, and in a very weak condition.

"I'll do what I can for him, sir, but I'm not very hopeful. He's in such a bad state," reported Mr McBride, the ship's surgeon.

"I know you will, Doctor," replied Merriman. "But if you can revive him and he can speak, I must know what happened to his ship."

An hour later the marine sentry outside the great cabin door knocked to announce Mr McBride. "It was no good, sir, I couldn't save him and he died a few minutes ago." reported McBride. "He only said a few words, sir, very disjointed, but I did manage to make some sense out of his ramblings. Something about French pirates, killing all aboard who resisted and taking the others for sale into slavery. They took what they wanted of the cargo before blowing a hole in the ship's side to sink her. He had managed to hide and only just managed to get into the sea before she capsized. The ship was his father's, only a small trader, sir."

"Thank you, Mr McBride, he will have to be buried in the sea right away. Pity we don't even know his name."

Two days later the wind fell away and *Lord Stevenage* was becalmed with only the occasional puff of wind, not enough to give the ship steerage way. The sun was blisteringly hot and, as usual, Merriman had the awnings spread to give much needed shade and relief for the men. Tempers began to fray and some men began to argue loudly and forcefully. The Boatswain and his mates had to use their starters, ropes with knotted ends, on several occasions. The surgeon had insisted that the crew all kept their shirts on to avoid sunburn but as usual some men thought they knew best and were badly burned. McBride spread some concoction on the sufferer's backs to ease the stinging but one man was burned very badly as well as becoming delirious with heatstroke so that he was confined to the ship's tiny sick-bay. His offence was recorded and when fit he would receive some punishment.

One evening, a loud scream from above brought Merriman racing on deck followed immediately by the off-watch officers. "What the Devil's going on, Mr Weston?" he asked the officer of the watch.

For answer Weston pointed aloft at the main yard arm where Smithers was hacking frenziedly at all the ropes he could reach. "He attacked bos'n's mate Gilbert, sir, stabbed him but I don't know how badly. Mr McBride's with him now, sir."

Merriman strode forward to see what the surgeon had to deal with and found Gilbert lying in a pool of blood flowing from a fearful wound in his belly.

"No good, sir, he's dead or as good as. I can't help him." As McBride spoke the man gave a violent shudder and was gone.

Merriman turned to the men around him. "What happened here? Who saw it?" he demanded.

Ted Jackson, an ex-poacher newly promoted to warrant rank said, "I saw it, sir. Smithers was throwing coils of rope off the fife-rail, sir. Gilbert ordered him to pick them up and he refused. Then Gilbert raised his starter and Smithers stabbed him and then climbed aloft, sir. Nobody was near enough to stop him, sir."

"Thank you, Jackson. Mr St James, I want your marines on guard at once and your best marksman with me on the quarterdeck."

In no time a line of marines in their scarlet jackets and white cross belts were standing behind Merriman. He raised his voice and shouted, "Smithers! Smithers, you have killed an officer, plain murder, I believe. Come down and give yourself up."

The man had stopped cutting ropes to watch the activity below him and yelled, "Like hell I will. All of you think you're better than me. What can you do? You won't shoot me. I'll show you!" He started hacking away again.

"So that's it then, Smithers, you force my hand. Mr St James, have your man shoot him now."

The Marine marksman raised his musket, cocked and fired it in one rapid movement. The ball hit Smithers in the chest and, with an almost comical look of surprise on his face, he toppled backwards down into the sea.

Merriman looked over the crew standing below him. "The man was a murderer and deserved to be hanged. Many of you saw him do it and aloft he was trying to damage this ship which might have endangered us all. Now let that be an end to it."

As he turned away an unknown voice amongst the crew shouted, "The bastard deserved it. You'll get no trouble from us, sir."

Down in the stifling air of his cabin, Merriman was regretfully considering what to write in the punishment book when the marine guard banged his musket on the deck and called, "First Lieutenant, sir." At Merriman's call to enter, Lieutenant Andrews came into the cabin.

"Yes, David, what is it?"

"A sad business, sir, but I have checked with most of the petty officers and they all report that there will indeed be no trouble from the men. The fellow was unpopular and the general feeling is that they are glad to be rid of him, sir. He deserved what he got and they don't like the other man, Greely. The bos'n and his mates are aloft and repairs to the damage that madman caused are nearly complete."

"Thank you. Obviously I shall have to put it in my report but I don't think anybody at the Admiralty will worry over it."

After Andrews left, Merriman fell into a mood of self-recrimination. It was my fault. The man was a trouble maker and I should have been more aware of it. Now it has cost the life of another man. Gilbert was a good man and a fine seaman. Damn it, perhaps I'm not good enough to be a captain? Another man would have seen this coming. And I had the fellow shot and killed when I might have found a different way. Damn and blast it.

Merriman paced back and forth across his cabin but he wanted more room and so he went up onto the quarter deck and paced up and down, up and down there, managing to subconsciously avoid gun carriages, shackles, coils of rope and other items. Seeing his glowering face, the officers and men assumed that he was in a rage and hastily moved over to the lee side to leave him alone with his thoughts.

What else could I have done? The man was a murderer and even if he had surrendered, his fate was sealed. There was no other course of action. Death is mandatory for murder as specified in the Admiralty's Articles of War, so why do I feel guilty of murder myself? I'll have it on my conscience for a long time to come I'm certain.

Suddenly he realised that everybody on deck was watching him pacing up and down and tugging at his ear, the unconscious habit he had when deep in thought. The officers were talking quietly and casting glances his way and the men at the wheel were trying not to draw attention to themselves.

"Has nobody got work to do? I'll soon find some for you. What about that main fore brace there? It's slack as the ties on a whore's drawers, are you all in a dream? One of you should have seen it, you're not attending to your duties. Now see to it," he snarled at them.

His seaman's instinct had noted the fault even in the middle of his deep and gloomy thoughts and, even as he spoke, he began to feel better as all hastily tried to look busy. Orders were passed and men ran to follow those orders. He smiled to himself. In fact with the lack of wind, the fore brace did not require much attention but it woke people up to see that their Captain missed nothing.

Night fell and after his supper Merriman retired to his cot and tried to rest. Sleep eluded him and it was near dawn before he managed to drift off for a few hours.

Chapter Five

Pirates attack & a thief onboard

Eventually cat's paws appeared on the sea and a light breeze sprang up but from the north which did little to help the ship's progress. Soon some lateen sails appeared on the horizon to the east and the masthead lookout with his telescope reported that they were dhows, four of them. All Arab ships and boats were called dhows by the English even though they were of different shapes and sizes. As their hulls crept over the horizon, the lookout reported that they were full of men and all flying a red flag on the main mast.

Merriman was finishing his meagre breakfast and his last cup of coffee when the hail drew his notice but made himself remain at the table. In only moments the marine guard called out, "Mr Midshipman Green, sir."

Green almost fell over his feet as he came in and excitedly gasped, "Mr Andrews' compliments, sir, and will you come on deck?"

He turned to run but was stopped by Merriman's voice. "Mr Green, kindly remember that you are an officer and stop rushing about."

On deck Andrews reported what was now clearly seen to the east. After using a telescope, Merriman thought for a moment then said, "Mr Andrews, I'll have the crew called to action stations, if you please, and have those awnings taken down. They may be pirates looking for easy prey or they may not but I shall take no chances."

"No doubt about it, sir, they are pirates. No peaceful trader would have such a lot of men aboard, and they all have a red flag at the main," said Andrews.

"Are they going to attack us, sir?" asked Alan Hungerford, the signals midshipman, hopefully. He stood in his proper place on the quarter deck.

"They may but I doubt it," replied Merriman. "They probably think they are going to attack an Indiaman but they'll change their minds when they find out we are a ship of war. They could be the ones that sank the trading ship we found."

Above the noise of partitions being dismantled and with furniture and chests taken down to the hold and the bustle of the crew doing all that was needed to prepare the ship for battle, Merriman stood on the quarterdeck deep in thought. *Is this to be our first taste of action against pirates and privateers in these waters, I wonder? We cannot manoeuver this ship with so little wind, whilst those fellows can. But what will they do? If they attack we will give a good account of ourselves.*

He took another look at the approaching ships and called out, "Mr Andrews, have the guns loaded with solid shot and grape but not run out yet. I'll have the courses off her shortly if these ships make to attack us, David, so have the Topmen ready."

The lower sails on each mast, the courses, were usually rapidly furled in the expectation of battle and the danger of fire. Merriman stood on the quarterdeck deep in thought, watching the activity around him. He took another look at the approaching ships, and then looked round the quarter deck again. Because of the heat, he had allowed the officers and warrant officers to leave their blue coats off, but he called the marine captain. "Mr St James, pass the word for the marines to hide themselves below. Your men in the tops should take their coats off. Red coats may frighten off these pirates, if indeed they are pirates, and I want to give them a nasty shock if they attack."

The four dhows approached and then split up into pairs, each pair changing course to pass by on either side of the frigate but closing nearer which would mean that they would attempt to board from both sides. There was now no doubt that the dhows were full of pirates, men shouting imprecations and waving swords and spears above their heads. A sudden crash of gunfire rang out as the biggest dhow fired a warning shot, the shot passing overhead and punching a hole in the fore topsail.

Many of the crew were cursing the pirates, "Come on you bastards, attack us, we're ready." The simpleton, Biggins, was jumping about waving a cutlass and shouting his hate of the French, indeed he did the same when any enemy ship appeared.

"Belay that noise down there," bellowed the first lieutenant. "You officers, can't you keep your men quiet?"

Merriman was watching the approaching ships with a keen eye, judging their speed. Then he shouted, "Top men aloft, get the courses in. Mr Green, get below and warn the officers that we shall open fire at my command, both batteries."

He waited a few moments longer looking down on the gundeck, seeing the officers in command there, Weston and Merryweather with their swords raised, then shouted, "Ready men, run out and fire as your guns bear."

The frigate showed her teeth as the gun ports opened and the black muzzles of the guns appeared. The leading ship, the largest of the four with a French Tricolour flying beneath the red flag at the top of the mast, immediately turned away. It was too late, and the frigate's full starboard broadside, the guns firing in turn as the enemy came in sight of each gun captain, hit the pirate ship hard. The main mast abruptly folded in half and the grapeshot tore bloody paths through the screaming men. On the larboard side, the guns almost blew the first of the two dhows into pieces with shot holes appearing at the water level. It immediately began to sink, slowly turning on its side with the crew sliding down the sloping deck into the sea. The remaining two moved away out of range of the guns, but not before some of the frigate's rapidly loaded guns scored some hits. They began to circle round, maybe in the hope of picking up some of their unfortunate fellows, but finally turning and sailing away.

Merriman called out, "That was well done, lads. Two of them are sinking and two of them are leaving but with this light wind we will never catch them. Mr Weston, have a boat lowered and see if there are any survivors. Keep the lookouts aloft and we shall not secure from action stations. It is beginning to go dark and there is no knowing what may happen overnight. Release the men by their sections in turn for food but they must stay by their guns. Mr St James, stand your marines down but keep them ready."

The ship's boat returned with only three rescued and terrified survivors aboard and Merriman ordered them to be secured below. Lieutenant Weston reported that there were no other survivors, only bodies with sharks rapidly disposing of them.

In the event, nothing happened overnight and, once the morning light had strengthened enough to see to the horizon with not a sail in sight, the men stood down from action stations and the normal routine of shipboard life continued. Then, early one morning as the watch was changing, before dawn light had begun to colour the horizon, a chorus of shouts and curses rang out from where the crew's hammocks were crammed together on the lower deck.

Lieutenant Shrigley, the officer of the watch, immediately sent a midshipman to the warrant officers' berth to bring them on deck. He walked along the starboard gangway almost to the fo'c'sle when a group of shouting men appeared below him with another man fighting and struggling in their grip.

"Belay that fighting, you men, at once. What is the trouble about?" He looked behind him to see the ship's Master at Arms Gillow and two of his corporals followed by members of the duty watch, all agog to know what was going on.

"Please, sir, we've caught a thief, sir. Caught 'im going through me mate's ditty box. Thought we were all asleep 'e did."

"Right then, Master at Arms, take charge of this man and put him where the others can't get at him. We'll have an enquiry later. You other men get below."

As the wretched man was led away, Shrigley realised that he was the other trouble maker, Greely, who came aboard with Smithers in Portsmouth, part of the motley gang of jailbirds recruited to make up the losses incurred in the affair with the French in Ireland.

As the dawn began to colour the sky, Merriman appeared on deck to take his usual morning walk on the quarterdeck. He strode up and down for the usual twenty minutes but all those on the deck knew his eye had missed nothing, from the compass bearing to the set of the sails and the state of the rigging. Lieutenant Shrigley had remained on deck even though he had been relieved by Lieutenant Merryweather as officer of the watch.

"Why are you still on deck, Mr Shrigley? Your watch has finished, has it not?"

"Yes, sir, it has but I wished to report a small matter to you. It happened only a few hours ago but I judged it not serious enough to wake you, sir." He related what had happened. "The Master at Arms has the man confined below, sir, he is that troublemaker Greely. I know you expected trouble from him but he is in real trouble now. Luckily we got to him before the men beat him senseless or worse."

One of the worst things a man could do aboard ship was to steal from his shipmates. A seaman had little to his name, only his knife and a few pitiful belongings important to him and kept in his personal ditty bag which was always normally regarded as private.

"Very well, Mr Shrigley. Have the Master at Arms bring him down to my cabin together with the witnesses. My compliments to Mr Andrews and ask him to come here. You must attend as well."

Merriman hated this sort of problem caused by one rotten apple among the crew but he knew he had to deal with it promptly. He also knew there was really only one punishment for such a crime. He was roused from his dismal thoughts by the thud of the marine sentry's musket thumping the deck.

"Master at Arms, sir." Merriman called for him to let the men in. The burly Gillow and one of the ship's corporals between them led in the miserable Greely, ashen faced, knowing what was likely to happen to him.

Merriman stared at him for a few moments then said, "I understand that you have been caught stealing from your shipmates. What have you to say for yourself? And look at me when I speak to you."

Greely lifted his head and the malevolence in his eyes shocked Merriman. "T'were'nt me, sir. I picked up the wrong ditty bag in the dark and they said I was stealing," replied the frightened man. "It was dark, sir, honest it was."

"Thank you. Mr Gillow, take him out and bring in the witnesses, one at a time."

"Aye-aye, sir. There's three on 'em, sir." He returned with the first man whom Merriman recognised as the ex-poacher Larkin, a man possessed of phenomenal eyesight.

"Now then, Larkin, tell me what happened, and no exaggeration mind, I want the truth."

"Aye-aye, sir, well it were like this. I had hardly been asleep for more than one or two hours, sir, when I woke, wanting to go to the head. I came back and saw Greely with his hand in another man's ditty bag so I shouted and woke some others and we grabbed 'im. 'e dropped something which we found; it was a piece of carving work and the only man who does that as good, sir, is the Welshman, Jones."

"Mr Gillow, what do you know about this?"

"Well, sir, this is Jones' work, lovely it is and I know none of the other men can do such fine work although they try." He placed the item on Merriman's desk. "Another thing, sir, I searched his bag and found four items which some of the men recognised and claimed, having thought that they had lost them."

The other two men could only corroborate what had been said though one man said that one of the items, a small pocket knife was his.

Merriman leaned back in his chair. "Thank you, Mr Gillow, these three men may go but keep Greely outside whilst we consider the evidence."

When they had left, Merriman turned to his two Lieutenants Andrews and Shrigley. "You have heard it all, gentlemen, what do you think?"

They spoke almost as one, "Guilty, sir. We know he was sentenced to deportation for stealing and chose to join the navy as the only alternative he had."

"Thank you, gentlemen, I agree and we know that there is only one punishment for that crime. Mr Shrigley, please have the prisoner brought back."

When Greely and his two guards were again standing before him, Merriman said, "Greely, there is no doubt of your guilt and you know the penalty for theft. You will receive twelve lashes and have to run the gauntlet followed by twelve more lashes as soon as it can be arranged. Take him away, Mr Gillow."

It was quickly arranged. A grating was fastened up to which the prisoner was tied and all hands were called to witness the punishment. Merriman stood at the quarterdeck rail with the officers, looking down onto the gun deck, seeing that most of the men had equipped themselves with short lengths of rope with a knot on the end.

"Men, you know what happens to a thief and I see that you are ready. Mr Brockle, you may begin."

Brockle, the boatswain, drew the lash from a red cloth bag and shook it out to ensure that none of the strings were tangled. At the first blow Greely squealed as red lines appeared on his back but suffered the next eleven lashes silently before being cut down, his back a bleeding mess. The crew, except for the necessary men on watch, formed themselves into twin rows on both sides of the deck each man ready with his piece of rope. Greely was pushed into his place with the Master at Arms in front of him holding his cutlass against his chest to stop him bolting and a corporal behind him to urge him forward with a sword against his back. Hesitantly he moved forward, prodded into movement as his erstwhile shipmates lashed at him with their ropes. By the time he had reached the end of the second line he was staggering with his eyes shut and with his back and shoulders red with blood before he collapsed face down. Mr McBride, the surgeon, examined him before calling up to Merriman, "He won't live through another twelve lashes, sir. I know it."

Merriman was not a cruel man and had watched with a face like stone as the punishment had continued. A horrified Midshipman Green had run to the side before being violently sick overboard.

"Very well, stop the punishment. Mr McBride, he is in your hands now. Mr Andrews, dismiss the men."

A bucket of fresh seawater was thrown over Greely, not as more punishment but to wash him down, the salt water also acting as a harsh form of antiseptic.

The following day a light wind arrived and rapidly increased to good strong wind on their port quarter. At Merriman's order, the officer of the watch sent the Topmen aloft to let fall the courses and, with men ready at the braces, sheets and bowlines, the yards were hauled round to the best point of sailing to take every advantage of the wind to make good their course north.

It was not long before the wind gained in strength and soon white-topped waves were breaking on the starboard side with even bigger ones in sight. Merriman crossed the deck to speak with the Master and Merryweather, the officer of the watch.

"What do you think, Mr Cuthbert, will it get worse?"

"Aye, sir, it will. These tropical storms have a nasty habit of coming out of nowhere and finishing just as quickly but they can be vicious and many a ship has lost its topmasts by leaving it too late to reef. Quite common at this time of year, it's called the monsoon."

"Thank you, Mr Cuthbert. Lieutenant, call all hands. I'll have all the t'gallants off her and a couple of reefs in the tops'ls. Get the courses off her again, we'll weather this under jibs and well reefed tops'ls. Does that suit you, Master?"

"Aye, sir, may I suggest extra lashings on the boats and lifelines along the deck."

The ship was beginning to roll and pitch and Merriman looked up to see the Topmen, like crows on a branch, desperately clawing at the main course as the wind increased. Eventually all was done but only just in time as the wind rose to a crescendo, shrieking through the rigging and, even under minimum sail, the ship heeled well over to larboard. The rain came down in sheets from the racing clouds overhead, blown sideways by the wind and all on deck were soon soaked to the skin.

The Master with one of his mates and three other seamen fought the big double wheel to try and keep on course but it was difficult and Mr Cuthbert shouted to Merriman, "Sir, I think we must just run before it without the fore and mizzen tops'ls."

No sensible Captain argued with a Master as experienced as Mr Cuthbert. "All hands, Mr Merryweather. I'll have the tops'ls off her."

Once again the Topmen clawed their way aloft, desperately clinging to every handhold as they fought their way out onto the yards, lying almost horizontally, their feet on the footropes with the wind doing its best to blow them away. At last it was done and as the exhausted men climbed down below, Merriman ordered that every one of them be given an extra tot of grog. He stayed on deck holding on to the weather shrouds, battered by the wind and rain and almost deafened by noise of the gale's violence.

Waves and clouds of spray came over the weather rail repeatedly, soaking him even more and making it increasingly difficult to see anything. With the violent pitching, the beakhead smashed into waves sending water cascading over the bows and the main deck whilst the few men whose duty kept them on deck clung desperately to ropes and anything solid. Merriman's cox'n, Matthews, tried to get him to wear a tarpaulin coat but he waved him away, shouting, "It won't help now, Matthews. I'm soaked already."

After only three hours, which had seemed like more, the wind abated, the rain stopped and the sun appeared low in the sky behind the racing clouds. It was as hot as ever and everything began to steam and dry. Merriman looked keenly aloft to see if his ship had sustained any damage. He saw that only one stay had parted and the boatswain was even then making his way aloft with his men to effect repair. All the officers appeared on the quarterdeck chattering about the severity of the gale until a bad tempered Merriman ordered them to be quiet.

"Mr Cuthbert, set a new course for Bombay then get below and rest. Mr Shrigley, I'll have all plain sail set again and report to me below if there is any problem."

A weary Merriman stumbled below to his cabin to find his two men waiting for him with towels and dry clothes. "I'm sorry, sir, there's no hot coffee yet, the galley fire has only just been re-lit. I'll fetch some as soon as I can," said Peters, his servant, as he and Tomkins, the clerk, helped Merriman out of his wet clothes.

"Never mind that now," said a weary Merriman before falling into his cot, asleep before he knew it. Peters gently covered him with a sheet before creeping quietly out of the cabin.

Chapter Six

A French Prisoner

Merriman blinked awake to find sunlight streaming in through the big stern windows. He stretched and listened to the usual creaks and groans of the timbers around him and the sound of bare feet on the deck above him, realising that he must have slept through the night. He knew that if anything had happened he would have been woken so for a few moments more he lay there in a contented doze, thinking of some quotation he remembered from somewhere: "Sleep that knits up the ravelled sleeve of care". It had worked and the next thing he knew was Peters standing over him with a big jug in his hand.

"Heard you moving, sir. Here's some of your favourite black coffee, your breakfast will be along in a minute."

Back on his feet and fully dressed and shaven, Merriman sat at the table to watch Peters laying out breakfast. True, it was nothing special, only a strip of fried fat pork and dry ship's biscuit crumbled and fried in the fat, but the smell of it reminded him that he was ravenously hungry. The food rapidly disappeared accompanied by more coffee and then a satisfied Merriman felt himself again, ready for anything.

The marine sentry outside banged the butt of his musket on the deck and called, "First Lieutenant, sir." The working day had started.

As Andrews appeared, Merriman told him to sit down. "There's still some warm coffee, David, if you want it, but tell me, is all well with the ship?"

"Yes, sir, all is well. When we could inspect things properly we found a few ropes badly chafed but nothing serious and they have all been repaired. If the gale had continued longer one of the cannon might have broken loose but that has been secured and the gun captain censured, sir."

"Very good, I'll come up. By the way how has Mr Grahame come through?"

"Seems to be alright, sir, he came on deck earlier. Apparently he has not suffered from seasickness as much as expected. Oh, and the Master says that we should be at our destination in only another two days. What do you want to do with the prisoners, sir? One of them is wearing the remains of a naval uniform, French I think, and is a white man, the other two are natives."

"Very well, David, have the Frenchman brought up to see me."

The prisoner in threadbare naval uniform, one Pierre Dumont, had been confined below decks in the same state as he was when rescued: wet through and apprehensive. The other two survivors, evil looking characters, were with him. All were shackled and closely guarded by two marines with fixed bayonets and who looked ready to use them at the least excuse.

Dumont thought back over the last five or six years since he became a pirate. He had been a lieutenant aboard a French frigate which attacked an English frigate in the Indian Ocean. Previously, his ship had captured a brig of which his captain had put him in as prize master. Stupidly, during the action against the frigate, he had got too close to the English ship, been boarded and barely managed to get back to his own frigate after being wounded in the arm by an English lieutenant. Now he was a prisoner of the English and likely to be hanged as a pirate.

His thoughts were interrupted by an officer who ordered the marines to take him on deck and escort him aft. The marine sentry banged his musket on the deck and called, "Prisoner and escort, sir."

Merriman pretended to be studying some reports on his desk and kept the prisoner standing for a good five minutes whilst the man became more and more nervous, casting glances around him, especially at his two marine guards. Finally, Merriman looked up and silently surveyed the man. His face seemed vaguely familiar and Merriman wondered if he had met the man elsewhere before.

"You are a French officer, I believe. Tell me why you have joined the pirates and why I should not have you hanged for piracy?"

"Oui, M'sieur. My name is Pierre Dumont and I have been pirate for quatre an... en anglaise, these four years since mon frigate Francaise left me and other wounded men in the Seychelles after a battle with an English ship. Mon capitaine told us he would be back for us later but the ship never came back and most of the wounded men died. I had nothing and I desperately wanted to go home but there seemed no other way to get enough money to pay for my passage home than to join the pirates. I was persuaded by a Dutchman, a pirate, who has many ships. He wanted me to join him because of my knowledge of navigation. He threatened to have me killed if I didn't join him but I was not really one of them. We thought your ship was an Indiaman."

"I see, M'sieur. You convict yourself out of your own mouth. You speak excellent English which seems to get better the more you talk. Why is that?"

"Ma mere est Anglaise, M'sieur. She taught me some English, but my father is French."

Merriman frowned. "Now I have to consider what to do with you, M'sieur. The other two men we rescued, what do you know about them?"

"Both are good seamen but both are torturers and killers. I know no more, sir."

Merriman was in a quandary. This man could tell him a lot about the pirates but he would have to be alive to do it, hanging him would not help. Rapidly he made up his mind.

"Marines, take this man back below to where he was and keep him there."

When they had gone he turned to Lieutenant Andrews. "David, what do you think? All three deserve to be hanged but the Frenchman could give us a lot of information and he could be useful. As for the other two I am minded to hang them immediately unless they could be of use, they are seamen."

"No, sir, I think they would only be trouble and we don't need them. I say hang them."

"Very well then. Have the bos'n rig two nooses at the main yardarms and have the crew on deck to witness."

That done, the two pirates were brought on deck and when they saw the ropes they knew what they were done for and fell on their knees babbling away in their own tongue as the nooses were put over their heads.

Merriman addressed his crew, "Men, you all know the penalty for piracy is death by hanging. We killed all those others and it is only fair that these two are sent to join their friends. The third man was an officer and can give us plenty of details about the pirates so I will keep him alive for now. Bos'n, do your duty."

Two teams of sailors rapidly hauled the two men aloft where, after several minutes of violent, desperate kicking and struggling, they died. They were cut down and plunged into the sea where the fins of sharks quickly appeared to dispose of the bodies.

Merriman spoke quietly to his lieutenant, "Very well, David, have the Frenchman released from his shackles, though only temporarily, mind. Have him fed and given water to wash himself but have him accompanied by two marines at all times. He may be allowed on deck twice a day but if he tries to escape when we reach Bombay he will be shot. Make sure he understands that."

Chapter Seven

First sight of Bombay

Merriman's first task on arrival at Bombay would be to report to the Governor of what was known as the Presidency and talk to the senior factors or agents of the East India Company. As his ship glided gently under tops'ls and jibs between the islands and into the bay he ordered most of the sail off. He saw other warships at anchor, obviously those of the Bombay Marine because they were all showing the East India Company's own flag of red and white stripes with a small red St George's cross overlying the blue saltire of Scotland at the peak. A frigate, the *Bombay*, was the largest with five smaller ships close by, two small brigs, two sloops and what was known as a bomb ketch, a shallow draught, two-masted vessel with a mortar placed in front of the mainmast. All appeared to be smartly kept and Merriman was pleased with his first impressions. Many merchantmen including two large Indiamen were scattered at anchor.

He was so deep in thought that the crash of cannon startled him. Of course it was the usual salute fired as a ship arrived and Merriman grinned as he pictured the gunner walking along the gun-deck reciting the old ritual: *"Number one gun - fire. If I wasn't a fool I wouldn't be here. Number two gun - fire. If I wasn't a fool..."* The phrases were intended to keep the correct timing between each cannon shot. As he finished the salute the cannon in the forts high on the hillside replied in kind.

Turning to Andrews, Merriman said, "I'll have the anchor party ready and prepare to back the fore topsail..."

He shut his mouth and cursed his own inattention as he saw that Andrews had already done this. At his order the crew began to haul on the sheets and bowlines to swing the fore topsail yard and sail through the eye of the wind, the sail flapping before the wind pressed it against the mast to face the light breeze to act as a brake. That done, most of the way came off her and as the ship stopped and began to move backwards, Andrews shouted the order to drop anchor. Once it was down and cable paid out and stopped, Andrews and the Master took bearings on dominant features ashore to ensure that the anchor was holding. Once certain, he reported to Merriman that all was secure.

"Very good, Mr Andrews, have the awnings spread again."

Bombay was a sprawling town covering several islands. Most of the buildings were whitewashed with a few painted in colour. With the bright sunlight sparkling off the small wavelets, it was all an eye-squinting glare of light.

Knowing what his captain would want, Merriman's cox'n Matthews had his barge in the water almost before way was lost, with the boat's crew dressed all alike as their captain insisted. Indeed those clothes had been provided at Merriman's own expense to create a good impression on whoever was watching. Merriman's own father, a former frigate captain, had impressed on him the need to present as smart an impression as possible. It also bespoke an efficient and competent ship.

"Matthews, I want to pass as close as possible to that frigate. We are here to fight alongside it against pirates so I must see how wide awake they are."

As they passed an officer showed himself on the quarterdeck and raised his hat in salute. Merriman raised his own hat in acknowledgement and took in the ship's details with a critical eye. The boat quickly reached the quayside and Merriman, Andrews and Mr Grahame stepped ashore on some stone steps leading up to a wharf. The oppressive heat had them sweltering in their heavy coats as they looked about them with interest. Merriman instructed Mathews to take the boat back to the ship and wait for his signal.

A smart carriage with an Indian driver was waiting and a man came forward to greet them.

"Good afternoon, gentlemen. I am the Governor's secretary, Morgan by name but I assure you that I am not related to that notorious pirate." He laughed at his own joke and then continued, "We saw you arrive and the Governor sent me with his carriage to meet you."

On the drive they looked around them in astonishment at the curious sights of an Indian town and the miscellany of people. There were women in bright-coloured saris walking with servants following, and half-naked and barefoot coolies busy unloading trading vessels and doing menial tasks such as brushing the roadway and carrying all manner of boxes and bundles of trade goods. Scruffy urchins held out their hands for money, and on every corner, or so it seemed were beggars, blind or maimed in some way, pitifully holding out their hands for the small coins that the better off of the passers-by might be disposed to throw to them. A mass of humanity all going about their own business with the hotchpotch of smells from market stalls and cooking fires barely concealing the smell of rotting food. All this mixed with the stench of human and animal waste.

As the carriage approached the main fort they could see cannon poking out of the embrasures on the top of the walls. As they passed through the gates in the defensive walls, the native soldiers standing guard saluted smartly. Inside were bigger buildings which appeared to be as solid as could be found in an English town although with Indian ornamentation. Behind those buildings could be seen the bungalows of the senior factors and merchants. And beyond and outside the wall could be seen the lesser houses of the company clerks and the shacks of the native population, again built inside another wall.

The carriage pulled up under the large portico of a big building which Morgan told them was Government House, the Governor's residence and office. Once inside, Morgan ushered the three men into a large, cool room decorated in Indian style with wide open windows covered by jalousies to keep the sun out. Two large punkahs or fans operated by unseen natives by means of thin string kept the air stirred and fresh.

The Governor rose from behind a huge desk and came forward to welcome them. "May I present Captain Merriman, Lieutenant Andrews, sir, of His Majesty's ship *Lord Stevenage* and Mr Grahame. Gentlemen, Governor Jonathan Duncan."

"I can't tell you how delighted I am that you are here, gentlemen, though I confess I had hoped for a three-decker at least. Morgan, please call for refreshment for our guests. Sit down, gentlemen, and take off your heavy coats if you wish. In this heat we don't stand on ceremony too much." As they thankfully removed their heavy garments, the Governor continued, "And now please tell me all the news from home in England. Did you have a good voyage and what is your role in all this, Mr Grahame?"

"An uneventful journey, sir," said Merriman, "but slow. Except that we had a brief encounter with some pirate vessels. We sank two and the others fled. Also we found the wreck of a small trading ship off to the north of the Seychelles Islands, upside down with only a boy clinging to the keel. Unfortunately he died before he could say more than they had been attacked by a French pirate ship. I am sorry to bring you such bad news and I'm sorry to disappoint you, sir, but my ship was all that the Admiralty could spare. Of course you know that we are still at war with France and the fleet is stretched to the limit with blockade duty, escorting convoys from the West Indies and seeking out our enemies in so many places."

"I'm sorry in my turn, Captain, I meant no disrespect but the situation here is getting worse and I don't think a three-decker or even two would be too many to deal with these damned cutthroats who are preying on our ships. They even land ashore and go far inland in search of loot and slaves." He broke off when an Indian khitmatgar or servant appeared with a tray of tea and biscuits which he placed on a small side table. After serving them he disappeared and Morgan sat with them eager to hear their news.

"Well the news could be better, sir. Bonaparte's armies are crushing all opposition before them in Europe and seem impossible to defeat. We are holding our own at sea but on land we seem to be in a hopeless position. Napoleon wanted to invade Britain and the navy was all that stopped him. Mr Grahame, perhaps you will relate to the Governor what we know about Napoleon's plans for India."

Grahame did so. A shaken Duncan, his face going paler and paler as the news unfolded, gasped, "What a diabolical plan. One must admit that this fellow Napoleon is something of a genius and a persistent threat to us all. As Shakespeare said about Caesar, 'He doth bestride the world like a Colossus'. If he is as good a military leader as we have heard, I think that we in India would be hard pressed to stop him, even if we could gather all our troops together and various maharajah's armies. It doesn't bear thinking about."

"There is another serious matter I am to investigate, Governor," said Grahame. "Even back in England we have heard rumours that Tipu has determined to construct a large fleet in massive dockyards along the Malabar Coast but we don't know which they are. We know, as you will know, sir, that Tipu, the ruler of Mysore, has managed to subdue all the petty kingdoms in the south west of the country which gives him access to and possession of all the best ports and dockyards there."

"Yes, we know that he is still trying to expand his lands and we do know that he has ports in his hands, Mr Grahame, but I know nothing about a fleet. Although, as you say, rumours are flying about. I considered them to be nothing more than the usual native gossip but from your news it will have to be taken seriously," replied the Governor. "I have spies everywhere, sir, mostly unreliable, I must admit. They have told us of Tipu's conquests but nothing about a fleet."

"Well with all we know, it seems that Tipu is bent on another war, in spite of having been beaten in three wars already," said Grahame. He paused. "Another item I must report back to London, sir. What your directors in London are desperate to know is the capability of the Company's army, how many troops you have got and how well trained they are? Will there be any serious interruption of trade and is there any likelihood of Bombay falling to Tipu's forces?"

"As for other news, sir," broke in Merriman. "I know almost nothing. As usual Parliament is talking and arguing without deciding anything. I believe our country's saviour there is the Prime Minister Mr Pitt. Some of them are even talking of arranging an armistice with Napoleon, almost treason if you ask me. The country probably needs my ship in the Mediterranean as much as you need it here to defeat the pirates. Another point, sir, frigates can take to shallower waters than a three decked ship could and I do know that the seas around Oman are quite shallow."

"Very well, Captain, we must make the best of what we have. May I propose that we meet again tomorrow, with the captains and officers of the Bombay Marine ships and the leading factors of the company to talk through the possibilities of what can be done. I think it would be best in the evening when the heat has abated somewhat and I will entertain you all to dinner and we can talk afterwards. It will enable you to meet everybody that matters here and to form your own opinions about our Marine officers."

"Thank you, sir, that will be ideal, but before then are you able to supply my ship with fresh water and food? I have kegs for water and plenty of well-scrubbed barrels for meat. If you can supply the ship with cattle, sheep and pigs my men can butcher them and salt the meat down. Oh, can you supply salt for that purpose?" Merriman considered what else would be needed to keep the ship independent of the shore for as long as possible. "Also we shall need flour for bread making, hard biscuit and plenty of oranges and other fruit to keep my men healthy. Salt fish perhaps and fresh vegetables, eggs and some live chickens. Can you supply all of that, sir?"

"Indeed we can, Captain Merriman, and I will issue orders immediately so that the work may commence at dawn tomorrow. We can supply rice also and several different herbs and spices if your cooks can use them. Come to think of it, you could send one of your cooks to my kitchens to learn about what I imagine your crew will call funny foreign food. If you can bring your ship alongside the wharf, the work would be easier done. The harbourmaster will show you where."

Chapter Eight

A desertion

Dawn was only just breaking, with its customary rapidity, but the crew was already hard at work unloading casks and barrels onto the wharf with the aid of tackles rigged to the yardarms. Mr Duncan was as good as his word and coolies were there with carts ready to help. A watering party set off to where fresh water was available with a reliable petty officer in charge and the carts loaded with the empty casks. As they left, more wagons and carts began to arrive on the wharf loaded with tubs of various sizes containing flour, salt, rice and bundles of herbs and vegetables and sacks of fruit.

The purser, Mr Grummage, took charge of the loading, counting everything that was taken aboard, with an officer and petty officers keeping their eyes open for thievery and bad quality. Tomkins, the clerk, kept his own notes and totals.

A messenger arrived to say that the livestock was assembled for slaughter behind the town. So again, a working party set off with knives and axes, salt and barrels. The purser's mate was in charge of them as he would have to keep a record of everything.

Mr Morgan appeared on board as Merriman and Grahame finished their Spartan breakfast. He climbed down the companionway, crashed his head on an overhead beam and told the marine sentry who he was. As he rubbed his head the marine sentry announced him, "Mr Morgan, sir."

"Good morning, Captain, the Governor sent me, sir. He knows that you will have a lot of questions about affairs here in Bombay and the pirates and I am to do all I can to help you."

"Well, Mr Morgan, first of all I need to know more about Bombay before we talk about the pirates you are troubled with. I do know that it was a Portuguese and then a Dutch trading post and that the company moved here from Surat in sixteen sixty four or five, I think it was. I believe the fort was built in sixteen sixty five. The French had great influence out here with their own East India Company but I understand that has closed down."

"Yes it has, it was liquidated by the French Committee of Public Safety about six or seven years ago. We heard that some of the directors and deputies were executed for bribery and corruption. But French influence has been on the wane for years although many Frenchmen stayed here and intermarried with local women. And of course we have had frequent reports of pirates and the occasional French frigate in the Indian Ocean. On both the Malabar coast and the Coromandel coast, but nothing recently."

He paused to think, then went on, "As you heard from the Governor, there is trouble brewing inland in Mysore where the ruler Tipu Sultan, who calls himself The Tiger of Mysore, has an army trained by the French. He was always a keen ally of the French and indeed some of the French officers are still there, as I understand. We have had three wars with him and beaten him each time but I think there will soon be another. We know that Tipu is trying to make treaties with other rulers around his lands to encourage them to make war against the British, indeed he has virtually taken over control of most of the coast and lands south of here." He paused for breath. "We hope that the Company armies with a stiffening of British regiments can deal with them."

"I saw soldiers on guard at the gates. Are they company employees?" asked Merriman.

"Yes," replied Morgan. "We have our own army of grenadiers and light infantry. We call the ordinary soldiers Sepoys and the higher ranks have different names such as Naik or corporal, Havildar or sergeant, up to Subedar or Major. Most of them are higher caste Hindus. All the officers are British, trained at the Company's military academy in England. They are really very good. We are trying to recruit and train more here in Bombay because of the Tipu's warlike noises but if necessary we can call for soldiers from further away."

"Mr Morgan, I believe that Bombay is called a company factory. Do you manufacture anything here besides using it as a trading port?"

"No, nothing is actually made here; we call it a factory because the principal merchants and company officers are called junior and senior Factors. Below them are the clerks or writers who keep all the records up to date. I am also a Factor, sir. I have some small ships trading up and down this coast. My main warehouse is here in Bombay but occasionally I travel to deal with Indian traders. We do congratulate ourselves on having a fine Church, St Thomas Cathedral, which was built at the beginning of the century and it fact it was the first Anglican Church here. We also have two newspapers, the Bombay Herald and the Courier, tho' they are less than ten years old."

Merriman nodded, taking in all these details.

"Now, sir, if you have no further questions, I must tell you about the native quarter of the town."

"Oh, is there a problem with the people here?" asked Merriman.

"Only with some of them, sir. You should keep a good watch out for thieves, they can move about in the dark like shadows. We post sentries, Sepoys, on the wharves but somehow the thieves manage to avoid them. Quite a lot of stuff disappears in the night. When you have finished loading it would be better if you anchored out in the bay. Another thing, sir, your men. I saw many of them eyeing the native women as they walked past and it was obvious what the men were thinking. I know that they have been at sea for months but if they must have a woman, they should go to one of two particular brothels in the port. On no account must they wander about in the native quarter at night unless they want to be robbed and have a knife in the ribs for good measure."

"Thank you, Mr Morgan, I will issue orders to that effect and try to ensure that all my men are told what may happen to them if they disobey. One last thing, can you give me more details of this monsoon?"

"Indeed I can, sir. It is a regular seasonal feature that usually gets here in mid-June, coming up from the south. Gale force winds, heavy, almost torrential rain and when it really gets going, thunder and lightning. It usually arrives in the afternoon so regularly that one could almost set a timepiece by it. You will probably see children and even adults playing about in the rain in the streets, it is so welcome."

"Thank you, I think we encountered the beginnings of it before we arrived here. So thank you again, I must look to my ship to see that everything is in order and the new stores are being stowed correctly. I am sure that my officers will be overseeing everything but it is my ship and I must be certain. So, I hope to see you tonight at the governor's dinner."

By late afternoon most of the loading was done, the sailors working with a will in the strange situation and, as sailors always do, making friends with the coolies, giving them nicknames and treating them as though they were ignorant children. The only incident to mar the whole day was the disappearance of the man Greely, reported by the purser's mate in charge of the butchering of the animals.

"He's run, sir. We couldn't find him and with dark coming on I thought I should get the men back on board."

"Thank you, you did right. That will be all." Merriman turned to Lieutenant Andrews saying, "That man has been trouble since he came aboard and I am minded to let him go and mark him down as 'run'. He'll probably turn up dead, floating in the harbour with all the other rubbish, dead dogs and such like. He brought it on himself and I am not going to risk sending men out in the dark to find him."

As the light faded Morgan arrived in the Governor's coach and Merriman and three of his officers, all dressed in their best uniforms, with Mr Grahame, prepared to leave. The third officer, Lieutenant Merryweather, was left in charge of the ship and the loading party who continued to work by the light of lanterns. A marine guard was posted on the quay.

Chapter Nine

Trouble with a trader

At the Governor's residence, the entrance and the hall into which the party was ushered were ablaze with the light and heat of countless candles and lanterns and all looked around them with curiosity. But there was no time for chattering as Governor Duncan, surrounded by elegantly dressed ladies and gentlemen, advanced to meet them. After the endless bowings, curtseying and introductions had been done, Merriman introduced his lieutenants Andrews and Weston, the Marine Captain Edward St James and Mr Grahame. St James as usual caused quite a stir amongst the ladies. There was a busy fluttering of fans by the ladies in the excitement of having the rare presence of new faces amongst them and the men were soon surrounded by ladies eager to hear the news from home.

The officers of the Bombay Marine ships were keeping themselves somewhat detached from the rest of the visitors and Merriman began to wonder what effect his arrival would have on the captains of those ships. He knew that even though he was at the bottom of the Admiralty's list of Post-Captains, with less than three years seniority, as the captain of a frigate of the British navy he would take precedence over the officers of country ships, even over the captain of the Company frigate who was otherwise the senior officer. Merriman knew that he was an outsider and probably only tolerated because they needed his help.

His thoughts were interrupted by a lovely young lady with an ample bosom fluttering her eyes at him on one side and on his other side by an older lady that Merriman realised was the governor's wife.

"Come come, Captain," she said, "I see that you are deep in thought but as you are the guest of honour I claim the right to ask you to be my escort into dinner. Our Khansamah has indicated that it is ready. Oh dear, Captain, don't look so confused. A Khansamah is a butler. You will soon get accustomed to the words we use here in India." So saying she took his arm and the younger lady attached herself to St James and they proceeded into another magnificent room followed by the rest of the company.

The meal passed in a whirl. So many different dishes were placed in front of them by a host of servants that he couldn't really say which was best. He took a large mouthful from a particularly attractive-looking dish and immediately his mouth felt as if it was on fire. He gasped for breath, his eyes watered and he grabbed his wine glass and drained it at a gulp. The Governor's wife roared with laughter as did some of the other guests near enough to see.

"Oh my goodness, Captain Merriman, I should have warned you about that one. It is the strongest flavoured curry one can have, too strong for me but many people love it," she said, motioning to a khitmatgar who was hovering behind them ready to fill Merriman's glass with more wine.

"I confess it is not to my taste, my lady. In the navy we rarely have the opportunity to indulge in such dishes." He gestured lower down the table to where his lieutenants Weston and Andrews were sitting, both red in the face gasping and coughing. "I think my officers also have been too quick to taste that dish."

Conscious that he must keep a clear head for the discussions to follow later, he asked if they could have something long and cold to drink. Seconds later a tall glass of orange juice was placed in front of him which he drained in one long draught. The glass was immediately refilled. The meal progressed but Merriman made sure to ask advice before trying any of the other local dishes.

Finally, after the Loyal Toast to the health of King George and many other toasts had been proposed, one by Merriman to the assembled company and especially to the Bombay Marine with whom he would be working, the ladies retired and left the men to their brandy and cigars. He realised that he had said the right thing as pleased glances and smiles came his way from the

Marine officers. The captain of the frigate *Bombay,* an elderly man by the name of Egerton, unbent enough to offer Merriman a rather wintery smile but the other officers seemed to be quite friendly.

Brandy and cigars were served by the khitmatgars who were immediately dismissed afterwards. After the men had taken a few appreciative puffs at their cigars and tasted the brandy, the Governor rapped on the table for silence.

"Gentlemen, you all know the reason for this gathering is to welcome Captain Merriman and his officers. Now his ship is here, what we must do is to try and devise some kind of plan to avoid any more of our ships being attacked by these damned pirates."

"It's not talk we need, it is action," shouted a portly, red-faced man. "We ask for help from England but what do we get after months of waiting? One solitary frigate and that's all. What can we do with that? We all have ships waiting for a convoy to be assembled for safety. The bigger Indiamen are fairly well armed and many have managed to sail and take the risk, but they won't wait for a slow convoy. All we have are two solitary frigates and one of those has gone gallivanting to Madras. The rest are small brigs and sloops which have been proved useless, so what more can another frigate do…?"

His voice was drowned out by the crash of Captain Egerton's chair going over as he leapt to his feet. "Useless, useless, are we? Damn it, man, I resent your tone. We do the best we can with our limited means. The Company is mean with its money and we are short-handed and short of many of the items needed to keep our ships in fighting trim." There were murmurings of agreement and support from the Marine officers.

The Governor shouted for calm and said, " Mr Goldberg, I know that you and the rest of you gentlemen have your problems and are in desperate need of getting your goods to England and other goods back to here, but recriminations will not help any of us so please keep silent. Perhaps Captain Merriman has something to say?"

Merriman rose to his feet, looked round the table at the well-fleshed men, most of whom had consumed a goodly amount of alcohol and were red-faced and sweating freely. He said, "Gentlemen, I do understand your problems but as you know I have only just arrived. I have no detailed information about these pirates and their depredations and until I do there can be no plans made. This must be a naval business and therefore I would like to invite all you senior officers of the Marine to come to my ship midmorning tomorrow for a conference."

"Very good, Captain, I look forward to that. I hope you have some fine wines aboard for us all?" said Mr Goldberg.

"I do, sir, but you will not be there. As I said, this is a naval matter and only naval men will be there…"

He was interrupted by a rude and red-faced Goldberg shouting, "Not there, not there? Damn it, Captain, we are all involved."

Merriman raised his hand. "Very well, Mr Goldberg, if you are so insistent on being involved, I think I can find a place for you on the gun-deck. There is always a place for a willing volunteer."

There was silence for a moment then a great roar of laughter from the assembled company followed Goldberg as he hastily left the room.

Captain Egerton raised his glass and said with a broad smile on his face, "A toast to your health, Captain Merriman. That man has been a perfect nuisance to us all and it was a delight to see him put in his place so deftly."

"Well, sir," replied Merriman, "there is an old saying which may be apt at the moment: 'Every ass likes to hear himself bray'."

More gales of laughter followed with Egerton and his men leading the noise with broad grins on their faces.

After the toast had been drunk and the excitement had died down Merriman said, "Gentlemen of the Marine, I look forward to greeting you on board my ship."

Chapter Ten

Conference with Bombay Marine Officers

The following morning, loading having been completed, the *Lord Stevenage* was moved to ride to her anchor in the wide bay. Awnings were rigged to provide shade for all on deck and the crew fell to working on the hundreds of jobs needed to keep the ship up to fighting trim. Men were high aloft checking every rope and stay. The sail maker and his mates were stitching a suspect sail while others were cleaning the guns.

Shortly afterwards, several boats were seen carrying the Bombay Marine officers to the meeting. Merriman met them all as they came aboard, with all the usual ceremony due to captains the world over. The visitors were wide eyed as they took in the sight of the immaculately holystoned decks, the gleam of brass work, the marine honour guard in their red coats and glaringly white cross belts. Not a rope was out of place, the hammock nettings full with not a single hammock badly stowed. The leathern fire buckets were well-polished and every detail of the ship was exactly as it should be. Merriman was pleased by the reaction from the visitors as he shook hands and ushered them below, past the marine sentry and into his cabin.

Once they were all settled as comfortably as the space allowed and the excited chatter had died down, Captain Egerton spoke, "Captain Merriman, sir, may I congratulate you on the condition of your ship. I know the King's Navy is keen on its cleaning and polishing but I have never seen better anywhere, even in my short time as an officer in your navy. I only wish we could keep the Marine's ships as smart but at least the crews are as well trained as we can make them, although I don't think our sail handling could match yours which was impeccable."

"Thank you, Captain, we do our best," replied Merriman.

Egerton continued, "I should like to introduce these officers to you, sir. Of my ship the *Bombay* there are Lieutenants

Wilde and Groom, of the sloops *Clive* and *Villain* Lieutenants Anderson and Johnson, and of the brigs Lieutenants Little and Oliver. We also have the bomb ketch you have seen, the *Little Thunder,* with Lieutenant Barton in command. We do have another frigate, the *Madras,* but it has been dispatched to Calcutta with the officer commanding our army. It was thought safer for him than going overland with all the troubles there."

"Very good, you are all welcome, gentlemen. I think you know my First and Second Lieutenants Andrews and Weston and the other gentleman is Mr Grahame representing Mr Pitt, the Prime Minister."

The officers looked at Grahame with interest.

Merriman called his hovering servant Peters to serve tea to all, aided by Merriman's clerk Tomkins. "I am serving tea for now, gentlemen, something stronger will come later." When the two men had finished and disappeared he continued, "Now then, I must know as much as possible about these pirates, their methods, the places from where they operate and when. In short, everything you can tell me. Have you had the good fortune to fight any out at sea and how did your crews behave in a fight? Are your crews a mixture of European men and Indians? I cannot begin to make plans until I know as much as you can tell me."

"To answer your last question first, Captain, most of the crew are Indian, with a stiffening of English and Dutchmen. The officers and petty officers are all English. Regrettably we have not had much luck at fighting the pirates; they generally have faster ships than ours and can slip into shallow waters where I cannot go with my ship. Our smaller ships can stand closer in but are usually outgunned by two or three pirate ships together. They use fast Arab ships we call dhows, although they have different native names, together with a few captured European merchant brigs, and they usually work in groups of anything from three or four up to six or seven. However, most of them have only a few cannon. They depend on boarding their prey. Our men have done well in the few skirmishes we have had, but most of them have never been in a real battle. In fact, when the pirates see my frigate they keep well clear and, being faster and of shallower draught than me, I cannot close with them," said Egerton regretfully.

"Thank you, Captain, all clear so far. Where do they sail from and what are their crews like?"

"It seems as though there are three areas where they raid from, sir. First is the Gulf of Oman, east of the Arabian Peninsula. The coast of that area is shallow and sandy with many small islands where we are at a disadvantage. They lie in wait at the entrance to the gulf where it is narrow and where they can attack and capture trading ships. Another area is on the western tip of the Arabian Peninsula leading up to the Red Sea from where they can lie in wait for ships filled with pilgrims for Jeddah and Mecca, and loaded with silver and gold. That area is important to the Company as trading ships from here and many other ports in India and further east trade all along the Red Sea and up to Suez. They have taken some of our Company ships, Portuguese ships from Goa, and many independent traders, but they don't seem to come too close to here."

Merriman nodded.

Edgerton went on, "I believe some have lairs on some of the bigger islands off Arabia, the Kuria Muria islands and Socotra to name but two, and many other small ports from where they attack ships far out in the Arabian Sea bound from India to Cape Town. Those pirates are mostly Arabs, although we know that some French and other Europeans are involved."

Egerton paused for a moment and asked if he might have another drink, then he continued, "Then there are the Seychelles Islands which gave aid and trading facilities to the French navy when it was here. We believe that some European pirates sail from there, French and Dutch mostly with a mixture of European, Arab and African crews. We rarely have much trouble with them. But the worst pirates, and those we have the most trouble with, are based somewhere south along the Malabar Coast, and the Maldive Islands. Most of the ones we have seen all fly a red flag. We do know that they are controlled by a Dutchman based somewhere in that area, a fellow by the name of Den Bosch, I believe, but he moves around. The Company is gathering merchant ships together to form a convoy which is why all the available ships we have are here to guard them on the voyage south. So you see, Captain, we are totally outnumbered with the few ships we have."

"I had no idea it is as bad as that, Captain, but I can confirm that at least one Frenchman is involved." Merriman told them about the small force that had intercepted his ship but which was quickly disposed of. "There was a man in the remains of a French Lieutenant's uniform aboard the biggest of them. I have him captive below and I hope that he will give us more information. If he can't, or won't, he will be hanged. Have any of you other gentlemen anything further to add? No? Then from what you have told me it is obvious that we cannot hope to cover all that vast area and we must concentrate on the nearest to here to begin with. Do you have any charts of the seas round this coast that may be more detailed than mine? If so my Sailing Master would appreciate seeing them."

Merriman paused then bellowed, "Peters, I'm sure our guests would appreciate a glass of wine. Have we still got any of that French wine that you found aboard *The Fat Frog?*"

"No, sir, it's all gone but we have your own, sir, well chilled in the bilge it is, sir."

He fled to fetch it whilst one of the captains said, "I'm sorry, sir, but what is *The Fat Frog?*"

The others leaned forward expectantly so Merriman had perforce to tell them about the affair in southern Ireland and the discovery of the wine.

"Nobody could pronounce the name of the French transport ship we captured and some wag on the lower deck christened it *The Fat Frog,* the name stuck. I have enjoyed that captain's stock of wine ever since. If you want to know more my own officers will tell you."

The officers sipped at their wine with several appreciative comments after which Merriman asked Grahame to tell the men what was known about the French intentions in Egypt and beyond.

"Thank you, James, I have a lot to tell you all but much of it is conjecture and I must find out more to be certain. Napoleon is massing troops and a fleet to invade Egypt, that much is definite, and his ultimate plan is to cross to the south of that land and find a fleet to bring him here to join up with Tipu Sultan in India. Our agents have confirmed all this, but what remains to discover is what Tipu is doing to help Napoleon. Rumour has it that he is going to build a big fleet. That is why I am here, gentlemen, but no word about why I am here must leak out. Spies are everywhere. I also emphasise to you all that what we are about must not pass to anyone else."

There were gasps of shock and a few white faces as the full import of the news struck them. Merriman drew the proceedings to a close.

"Gentlemen, I must have some time to absorb all you have told me, as you will about the French. I suggest we meet here again tomorrow morning. If you have any further ideas or plans we can discuss them then. I will show a signal when I am ready."

Chapter Eleven

Indian guide provided

The next morning, the Governor's carriage was seen on the wharf with Mr Morgan waving vigorously to attract attention. A boat was sent for him and Morgan was soon on board with another man, an Indian swathed in white robes who was introduced as Gupta.

Leaving him on deck, where he settled himself cross-legged on a mat in a corner, Merriman and Morgan went below.

"Now then, Mr Morgan, who is Gupta and why have you brought him here?"

"He lost his wife, parents, and his goods to the pirates. He wants to help us. He says that he knows many of the places along the Malabar Coast where they hide or come ashore to trade. He speaks good English, sir. The Governor thought he may be of use to you."

"Thank you, Mr Morgan. I will speak with him directly you have left."

Morgan recognised the hint and made his way back to shore. Merriman called for the First Lieutenant and for Mr Grahame.

"Gentlemen, you will be wondering who the Indian gentleman is, I'm sure. We knew very little about the situation in India which is why he is aboard. The Governor seems to think that he will be useful to us. He knows some pirate hiding places and if nothing else he could be our interpreter."

Merriman sent word by the sentry outside his door to have the Indian gentleman come to his cabin. The sentry knocked on the door, "The Indian gentleman is here, sir."

Gupta peered hesitantly round the door then stood in front of Merriman's desk with his hands together in *Namaste*, the Indian sign of respect.

Merriman decided he had to have confidence in the man so he began quietly, saying, "Will you be happy with accommodation and our food aboard my ship, Mr Gupta?"

The man moved his head from side to side in what appeared to be his version of a nod. "Oh yes, Merriman sahib, all very fine. I have some rice too." He spoke English well but with the unmistakable Indian accent.

Merriman said, "You will be treated well and should have no trouble with my crew, Mr Gupta."

Gupta gave his nod again. "All very good, sahib, no trouble. My name is just Gupta, no need call me Mister."

Merriman studied him and asked, "Gupta, how do you come to be in Bombay and why are you aboard this ship? I need to know as much about you as I can so that I know how to use you."

The Indian shook his head sorrowfully and began, "I was clerk in the offices of the Honourable Company here in Bombay. I learn English at the missionary school when I was boy and we lived in a small fishing village many miles south of Bombay. Two years ago, village was attacked by pirates, my wife and old parents killed and I was dragged away to join the crew of the pirate ship as a slave. I quickly learn what to do or not to do, Captain beat me until I obeyed. He was the man that killed my wife." He broke off with a sort of sob, and then continued, "I remember where the pirate villages are, sahib, and where they keep their ships."

All three of them listened attentively to the man's narrative.

"A sad tale, Gupta, you have my sympathies. My ship and I are here to see what can be done to stop these pirates and privateers so I can see now why Mr Morgan told me you would be useful. Tell me, how did you escape and how did you get back here?"

"I was on ship attacking another village and I climbed overboard and swam to shore to warn them but I was too late. All dead except the men and women who had been taken as prisoners. I learn to sail when I was with pirates so when I found small boat I tried to sail to Bombay but was picked up by an

Indiaman bound for Bombay. I think they wanted to keep me as crew but again I swam for shore and I found a priest who sheltered me and then brought me back here to Bombay. He told my tale to official sahib who questioned me and said I must stay with Father Jones until they found use for me again as a clerk. Then Governor sahib found me and so here I am, at your service, sahib."

"So, you know or can remember where some of the pirates lie in wait, can you? That should be very useful. Tell me, why you are doing this?"

"I told you, sahib, they killed my wife and family so I hate them. And the company has been very good and kind to us."

"Thank you, Gupta, you can go now. I'll speak with you later when I have considered the matter more." The man left the cabin and Merriman said to his companions, "I believe he may be useful to us, so where will you put him, David?"

"Well, sir, I'll give him a hammock in the midshipman's berth but he may be happier on his mat on the deck. By the way, sir, I think he is a Christian and not a Muslim or Hindu," Andrews replied.

"Very good, David, I think it is time to have the Company officers back here so please fly a signal to that effect."

When all were assembled again, with Merriman's own officers and Mr Grahame present, Merriman called for silence. "Gentlemen, I have been thinking over all that you told me yesterday and I believe I have put the bones of a plan together. The Governor kindly sent a man to me by the name of Gupta who had been a prisoner and slave of pirates and who knows where some of their ships may be found at anchor. This is what I propose…"

As Merriman outlined his plan, broad grins creased their faces and they left for their own vessels leaving Merriman alone with Grahame to consider their next move.

"Sentry, pass the word for the First Lieutenant, please."

When the three of them were settled, Merriman said, "Gentlemen, I think the next thing to do is have our Frenchman in here for interrogation. Have him in, David, with his guards of course."

A very apprehensive Frenchman was brought before the three of them. They looked him up and down in silence as though judging him.

"Gentlemen," said Merriman, "we must decide what to do with this man. He is French and our enemy but what is worse, he is a pirate. Pirates are hanged. Lieutenant Dumont, what have you got to say for yourself?"

"M'sieur, my parents are very old and I want to see them and France again. We took many small ships but I didn't kill anybody. I managed to collect nearly enough money to pay my way home but I lost it all when you sank my ship. So now I have nothing."

The Frenchman was certain that he had met the English captain before and cudgelled his brains to think about where he had seen him. He let out a gasp then looked directly at Merriman and said, "I know you, sir, you must remember. Five years ago our ships fought and you wounded me. I thought I was winning but my foot slipped on blood and you nearly killed me." He touched his arm in memory.

Merriman nodded slowly. "Yes, I thought we had met before. I remember it now, you fought well and I was lucky you didn't kill me. But that was all long ago. Mr Grahame what do you think?"

Grahame nodded. "As a pirate he should dangle on a rope, but," here he paused. "He must know a lot about the pirates, maybe something about Tipu's ship building and I think that if he will help us we should keep him alive."

"And you, Mr Andrews, what do you think?"

"I agree with Mr Grahame, sir, but if he won't help or gives us false information he must be hanged."

Merriman turned to their prisoner. "Dumont, you understand what we have said, don't you? Tell us the truth and it might save you from hanging. You will be kept a prisoner under permanent guard, shackled at night, until we see what you will tell us. If you were still a French officer I would take your parole but you are not. Mr Grahame, will you be happy to question this man?"

Grahame looked at the worried Frenchman. "Yes I will, Captain, and he will talk if he knows what is good for him."

Chapter Twelve

First Successful Raid

Two nights later, after dark, a Company sloop slipped quietly into a small inlet some fifty miles south of Bombay. Gupta had told them about it then shown them where it was whilst the ship had passed by offshore in daylight as near to the shore as possible. That foray allowed every telescope aboard to survey the scene. There was a small village of whitewashed houses and a jetty to which three Arab ships were tied up side by side.

Merriman had wanted to see for himself what the situation was and insisted that Egerton had come with him. "That will be a start I think, Captain Egerton, but we must sail on as though we have no interest in the place and then come back after dark," he said.

In the dark, the captain of the sloop, one Lieutenant Anderson, cautiously brought his darkened ship inshore with a leadsman in the chains. They sailed as close as he dared into the inlet and anchored. The boat being towed astern was brought alongside and a crew of six men with the sloop's First Lieutenant Clarkson, climbed as quietly as they could down into it. They carried some mysterious bundles and a roll of slow match, then the boat slid away into the darkness using well muffled oars. Those left on board anxiously peered in to the darkness although they knew that at least two hours would pass before anything happened.

The boat was well into the inlet, creeping along as quietly and as slowly as possible until they could see the three dhows dead ahead. No lights showed on any of them and the village was feebly lit by only a few lanterns. A larger building at the far end of the place showed more light and Clarkson could hear the sounds of revelry from within, but there was no sign of anybody on shore or ship.

Clarkson whispered to his crew, "All clear, lads, give way slowly towards the middle ship and we'll do what we came to do."

The boat crept slowly forward until a seaman was able to seize hold of some of the elaborately carved decoration on the prow of the ship. Then, carefully working hand over hand along the gunwale, he brought the boat into the darkness between two of the dhows. They waited a few minutes to be certain no alarm had been raised before Clarkson slowly raised his head above the bulwark. He could see no sign of any guards. It took but a moment for him and two of the seaman to climb aboard with the bundles passed up by the rest of the men. They crept along the deck until they found a hatchway.

"Dawkins, you go below, quietly now, and see if there is anybody there."

The seaman disappeared below to appear again almost immediately to report, "Nobody there, sir, They must all be ashore."

Quickly the bundles were passed below and arranged as near to the centre of the ship as possible. The bundles contained combustible materials, oil, rags and a small keg of gunpowder which Clarkson arranged in a pile with the keg underneath. Gently he eased the bung out and passed the end of the slow match into the gunpowder, securing it with a bit of rag stuffed in the hole.

"Quietly, lads, back down to the boat, I'll deal with this now," he said, carefully unwinding the slow match leaving a good length lying on the deck away from the powder. Mentally he tried to work out the length required for the delay needed to let them get clear, then he cut it. His flint and steel and a handful of fine kindling soon produced a small flame which he applied to the match. Hastily climbing back to the boat he ordered the men to row away as fast as they could back to where the sloop waited.

They were well clear, the men rowing as hard as they could, none of them wanting to be close when the powder exploded. Indeed, Clarkson was beginning to wonder if the slow match had gone out when it exploded with a great roar and a flash. The men could see the deck of the dhow split wide open and pieces of burning wood and other things raining down on the dhows either side. Those immediately caught fire, their tinder dry wood and tarred rigging blazing up in moments.

On the sloop, the watchers both heard and saw what happened but had to wait until the boat appeared out of the darkness, pulled alongside, and Clarkson and his men clambered aboard all with big grins on their faces.

"Went like a dream, sir," he reported to Merriman and Egerton. "I don't think anybody even saw us and I believe all three dhows are destroyed. Perhaps they will think it was their own careless fault."

"Well done, Mr Clarkson," said Merriman with relief in his voice. He turned to Captain Anderson. "If you would get under way now and get us as far away as possible before dawn, maybe the pirates will not even know we have been here."

There was great jubilation amongst the officers and Egerton congratulated Merriman on the success of his plan. "It's the first time we have been able to hit back, sir, I hope it will not be the last."

"I hope not too, but this was only a mere pinprick in the fleece of the animal, Captain. We must do considerably more than pinpricks in future."

The sloop sailed back into Bombay two mornings later and anchored. Merriman and Egerton were then rowed back to their own ships. Down in his cabin, Merriman slumped wearily into his chair and was nearly asleep when his servant Peters came in. "Breakfast Sir? Coffee maybe?" His cheerful voice grated on Merriman's ears when all he wanted to do was sleep.

"No, blast you, I must go to sleep," Merriman snarled.

"Very good, sir, your cot's all ready for you, sir," replied Peters, not at all put out by his master's bad temper.

Merriman staggered across the cabin to his sleeping space and collapsed face down on his cot. The last thing he knew was that Peters was taking his shoes off.

Chapter Thirteen

Next attacks planned

Next day, as the dawn's early light crept across the harbour, Merriman sat looking out of his cabin's great stern windows sipping at a mug of black coffee. Peters was hovering in the background, also with a fresh mug of the hot dark brew.

"Peters, pass the word to the marine outside for all officers and Gupta to report to my cabin in half an hour. Then you can shave me once I have finished this coffee."

At the end of the half hour all were assembled to find a freshly washed and shaved Merriman sitting at his desk with a large chart spread out in front of him.

"Good morning, gentlemen. I'm sure you are all desperate to know what happened the other night and what more we can do to deter the pirates." Merriman recounted the details of the action and that three dhows had been destroyed. Seeing smiles of approval all round, he continued, "Our friend Gupta said it was a place where pirates landed to trade their booty with local traders. Of course it may be that not all the dhows were pirate ships, but even so a blow has been struck against the pirates and those who profit from their activities. It was only a small but effective raid but it will be the first of many."

"Do you think that they know who it was that attacked them, sir?" asked Lieutenant Weston.

"We hope not, nobody was seen there and possibly they thought it was someone's careless fault that caused those ships to burn. Now then, our next raid must be far away from this one and hopefully the pirates will not connect the two."

Pleased smiles spread over the officer's faces at the thought of some action and little Midshipman Small piped up asking, "Will it all be small raids, sir, or will it be action involving this ship?"

"Maybe small raids to begin with, I think, but heavier raids in future to destroy as many pirate ships as we can. We know that there is at least one frigate with them somewhere and some Frenchmen. These are most likely to be privateers but the pirates have many bigger craft than we have seen so far."

"I hope my marines will have an opportunity to show what they can do, sir, they are itching for something more than drill," said Captain St James, the marine officer.

"I'm sure they will, Edward, but they will have to wait a little longer. So, that is all for now, gentlemen, you may all return to your duties except for you, Mr Cuthbert, Mr Andrews and Gupta."

Once the others had left, Merriman said, "Now, we must discuss where our next raid will be. We need to find another small place which Gupta will take us to but well away from our first raid in the hope that the pirates will not connect the two."

"I know place, sahib, lot of days sail further south from last time, bigger place and more ships will be there."

"Very well, Gupta, we'll try it. Can you pick it out on the chart? Mr Cuthbert, are your charts as up to date as possible?"

The Master spread a chart over Merriman's desk and all leaned over it. Gupta, not really very good at looking at or identifying items on a chart, took several minutes before he pointed with his finger. "I think it is that bay and river, sahib, but there are many bays and rivers and small inlets there."

"David, signal to the Marine ships if you will. All Captains and senior officers to be here in half an hour."

While waiting, Merriman's brain was working feverishly going over various plans for swift and silent attacks, which ships to use and how many.

When all were assembled in his cabin, Merriman said, "Gentlemen, I believe we have our next target. Gupta has identified a harbour well south of here. It would take perhaps three or four days to get there keeping well out offshore. It is a place called Karwar, well south of here. Do any of you know it?"

"I have sailed in that area, sir, on patrol as it were, but I cannot recollect seeing anything suspicious there," commented Captain Egerton.

Merriman turned to the silent Indian. "Gupta, what more can you tell us about this place Karwar, have you been there?"

"Yes, Merriman sahib. Many times I go there on pirate ship. Is a good harbour with much room, last time I saw maybe ten or twelve pirate ships tied up there. It is hidden behind a small headland and sand dunes which shelter the harbour behind it. I know they were pirates, sir, they all had red flags and they were trading with the people in the village behind. I think they go there many times; it must be one of their best hiding places. Some ships are built there."

"Very good, Gupta. Now then, gentlemen, what we must do is find out more about the place. Whilst the rest of us are keeping well out at sea and out of sight I suggest one of the sloops would be best for this. It could tow a small fishing dhow which, with one of your officers and a small crew of your Indian sailors and Gupta aboard, could land at night and in the dark find a suitable place to confirm what is there. I propose that your men do this, Captain, as being Indians they could pretend to be fisher folk."

Egerton nodded and Merriman continued, "From the chart I can see that there is deep water on the seaward side of the headland and if we can place our bomb ketch there at night to shoot over the headland it would give the pirates a nasty shock. If the place is suitable our marines could land and from the headland they could shoot down on the harbour. I suggest that all our ships go and with the sloops and brigs close inshore and the frigates lying off, we could cover the bomb ketch and deal with any pirate vessels that try to escape. Any comments, gentlemen?"

"By God, it could work, sir, and a use found for my little ship at last," said Lieutenant Barton, the commander of the bomb ketch gleefully. "We thought we had been forgotten and hoped we might be used. We are ready for anything."

"Very good, Lieutenant, I know that bomb ketches are slow and difficult to handle in bad weather, although I freely admit that I have no experience of them. What is the weight of shell that you can fire and over what distance? We are talking about a voyage taking three or four days or more, can you do it?"

"Yes, sir, we can. As you say we would be slower than the rest but I have no doubt we would get there. As for my large calibre mortars they can fire two hundred pound explosive shells about a mile to a mile and a half depending on the elevation and size of powder charge, sir."

"Good man. I think we should prepare to leave at dawn the day after next and sail off in a north westerly direction until we are out of sight of land, then turn south. For all we know there may be spies in the town here who pass information to the pirates and I do not want that to happen. You may trust your crews but one careless word could make a difference. I suggest that you tell none of them our plans until we are at sea. Captain Egerton, I presume the Governor will want to be informed so would you join me in seeing him? Secrecy must be our watchword so we must ensure that he has no servants near when we speak with him."

"Certainly I will, Captain, my thoughts are in line with yours. I have often wondered if somebody in Bombay tells the pirates what our ships are doing."

So it was that Merriman, Grahame and Captain Egerton were shown into the Governor's office by his secretary, Morgan. After the usual greetings had been exchanged, Merriman leaned forward and began.

"Mr Duncan, we have some news for you but before we tell you I would like to be sure that there are no other persons listening, servants or even sepoys, sir. We think it likely that there is somebody who passes information to the pirates."

The Governor looked surprised but sent Morgan to the door and he himself opened windows and peered out. ""Nobody outside, gentlemen. Morgan?"

"Nobody outside the door either, sir. All is clear and I sent the punkahs wallas away as well," declared Morgan.

Satisfied, Merriman began. "Sir, we have made one small but successful attack on pirates south of here and destroyed three of their ships. We have another attack planned which will keep us away for five or six days but there is another serious matter we must deal with first. As we know, there are many merchant ships waiting here in Bombay, desperate to sail for England. How soon can they be ready to sail in convoy?"

"I think only a few days, Captain. Most of them are already loaded but will need fresh water and provisions for a long voyage. What exactly do you propose, sir?"

"I propose that we take them in convoy well down south, perhaps a thousand miles or so and then return here. All ships except the bomb ketch and a brig will accompany them, but all captains of the convoy must know that any one of them that falls behind or shortens sail unnecessarily will be left behind. I believe that you have two big Indiamen ready to go. They are well armed and painted to look like frigates. If they could accompany us, sir, it would make our force appear stronger until we are past the worst pirate areas. Can you order them to do so?"

"Yes I can. The owners and captains will probably object but your plan promises even them with more safety than sailing alone."

"Excellent. Perhaps you could ensure that all the trading ships have powder and shot for their small cannon, sir, it could all help."

"Thank you, gentlemen. I will endeavour to have all ready by the time you return from your next adventure."

Chapter Fourteen

Attack on Tipu's Shipyard

Four days later, the small squadron was nearly at the designated target, the port of Karwar. This had been Portuguese but was now taken over by Tipu Sultan's forces. Careful navigation had put them at the point Merriman had chosen but well offshore. With all ships hove-to, he called all the captains aboard *Lord Stevenage* for a final meeting to ensure that all knew the parts they had to play.

Now, in the darkness, they moved closer inshore and hove-to once more. One sloop crept as close as possible before the captain, Lieutenant Johnson, sent the shore party off as arranged, under the command of Lieutenant Williams. The night was as black as pitch with only the faint glow of stars visible through gaps in the clouds. Almost two hours later and with no alarm raised, the boat re-appeared out of the gloom and the men climbed aboard.

"Well, well, how did it go?" demanded an impatient Johnson.

"No trouble at all, sir, there is a narrow beach backed by low sand dunes and then a bit of higher ground from where we could see the anchorage. There are about ten dhows there, mostly tied up together and there is a shipyard there with the part-built hull of what may be a frigate. An ideal target for our bombs, sir."

"Good, then show the signal."

A small lantern was with only a small gap in the shutter was raised up and down to the masthead.

Further offshore, Merriman waited in an agony of suspense for something to happen until a quiet word came from aloft. "Sir, signal light in sight, sir,"

"Mr Andrews, send the bomb ketch in, then the sloops and we will follow."

Careful and brief lamp signals, seen by all the other ships, set the plan in motion. Silently, the ketch moved in and soundlessly dropped two anchors with rope springs attached to the cables to help in positioning the ship. Then Lieutenant Evans and a party of marines were rowed ashore. It was Evans' job to find a place from which he could see the target and in the early dawn light using white flags could signal to the ketch the results of the bombardment.

Daylight was slowly beginning to pale the eastern sky when the first shot was fired. With a dull thud from the mortar, hardly heard offshore, the bomb was on its way over the low headland until an explosion signified that something had been hit.

High up on his ship's foremast, Merriman heard it and saw the flash. With Larkin, the crewman with the sharpest eyes on the ship, beside him and each with a big telescope, he was able to see all. It seemed to be only moments before the mortar fired again with another explosion following.

"Sir, flag from man ashore, sir. Traverse left."

Ashore, Lieutenant Evans had to remain hidden from the anchorage so as not to be seen. He had to be told by a concealed marine where the bombs had landed before he could signal the results. Two more followed in quick succession before the marine called out, "Sir, the beggars must know we're 'ere, sir. A mob of them are coming this way."

He stood up to see and shouted, "Right then, lads, get back to the boat as fast as you can."

He turned to go, then staggered and fell as a musket ball hit his shoulder from behind causing him to roll down the slope to the beach. The marines came leaping after him, grabbed him up and ran to the boat. As they piled in, the crew were already pushing it off and pulling hard on the oars. In the bows a small swivel gun was ready and a tug on the lanyard sent a hail of grape shot amongst the mob following. In no time they were back at the ketch as another bomb and then another was sent into the harbour.

"Your report, man," snapped Barton.

Evans, supported by two marines, drew himself up and said, "A success, sir, though I had hoped to hit more but they realised very soon where we were and came after us. I saw no other defences."

"Thank you, Mr Evans, now go and have your wound seen to."

All Merriman's ships had seen the results and began to close in to protect the bomb ketch according to the plan. Indeed, some dhows were beginning to appear round the headland and were making for the ketch which already had some sail up and with a man cutting the anchor cable. The nearest sloop and a brig immediately opened fire, the leading dhow was hit on the waterline forward and its mast collapsed. The second one tried to get past it but was struck hard and lost its own mast. Other dhows were trying to escape, spreading in all directions but to no avail as all the Company ships were spread out and waiting for them. None of the smaller Company ships had large cannon but the effect of so many shot striking home was devastating and when the frigates closed in those dhows that could turned back for shelter, pursued by one last broadside from the *Lord Stevenage*.

"A very good result, I believe," said Merriman when he heard the reports from the assembled captains. "Five of them were hit by the bombs from Mr Barton's ketch and sunk or set ablaze before they could be saved, and four more accounted for by the rest of us when they tried to escape. We have only one casualty in the whole affair. How is Lieutenant Evans, Mr Barton?"

"He'll be alright, sir, it was only a flesh wound and he's already boasting about being the only man in the action. But, sir, if I may comment, couldn't we have sailed in and finished the rest of them with little risk?"

"Maybe, Mr Barton, but we have no knowledge about defences there. Did any of you see any forts on the coast? No, neither did I, but I am reluctant to press home the attack without proper knowledge. We'll leave it for another time. So, gentlemen, we can all be satisfied with the results with special thanks to our tame bomb ketch."

There were satisfied smiles all round as the gathering dispersed to their own ships, a grinning Barton receiving many congratulatory thumps on his back.

Chapter Fifteen

Convoy planned & Agents sent

In the governor's mansion back in Bombay, a gleeful Mr Duncan was delighted with Merriman's report. "At last, at last we are hitting back, my dear Merriman. Where are you going next, or shouldn't I ask?"

"It would be better if you don't know, sir. Anyway we have not yet decided and the convoy is our next consideration. Is it all ready?"

"As ready as they will ever be, Captain. May I suggest that we have a meeting of all captains before you set sail so that you can ensure that they all know what will happen and they can be told and shown the meaning of your flag signals, sir."

All captains assembled the following day in one of the large warehouses on the quayside. Some of them were pleased to be going but others were grumbling about being held back by the slowest ships. The noise was rising when Merriman stood up and called for order.

"Gentlemen, we will sail at dawn tomorrow, wind and weather permitting. There are twelve of you and once we are at sea I want you to form yourselves into three columns of four so that your escort, including the two Indiamen, can most easily guard you. My Lieutenants will issue you with a suitable plan and also a list and drawing of signals you will see and which you must learn. Finally, and this is very important, any ship which falls behind through negligent watch keeping or shortening sail unnecessarily because of a captain's timidity, will be left behind. Is that understood?"

There were immediate shouts of protest, many captains shouting together with shouts of, "We can't sail as fast as a bloody frigate, you'll leave us behind," and "Why should anybody be left behind?"

Another captain shouted, "Why should we take orders from a Royal Navy captain instead of our own Marine captain?"

More shouts of approval followed those questions.

Captain Egerton stood up and raised his hand, waiting until the shouting had died down. Then he said, "Gentlemen, you all know me and you also know that the few ships the Company Marine has are not sufficient to fight all the privateers and pirates who might attack us. I am grateful that we have a frigate under the command of Captain Merriman with us. He is very experienced in these matters and I as the senior Marine officer I am happy to have him in overall command."

A roughly dressed captain shot to his feet and yelled, "Why should any ship be left behind? None of us can sail as fast as your ships except for the Indiamen. You'll all have to wait for us, I'm sure I have one of the slowest of all."

Merriman rose to his feet. "Captain, the convoy escort will include the two well-armed Indiamen and will stay close to the convoy except for one of the Company sloops which, being the fastest of us, will be ranging well ahead and to the side of us to give advance warning of possible attack. And why do you believe your ship to be the slowest? You are all very much alike and will carry the same amount of sail."

"Alike we may be, but if any spar is lost or rope work damaged it will take my crew a long time to make repairs, even if we can. We carry only small amounts of spare cordage and canvas, and it is nearly two years since the ship's bottom was cleaned"

"And why is that, Captain, who is your owner?"

"Mr Goldberg, sir. He won't pay what is needful for stores or cleaning, only the minimum he has to."

"I see. Captain Egerton, what do you know about this?"

"I believe he is right, sir. Mr Goldberg owns three ships in the convoy and will only pay for the cheapest repairs. It wouldn't surprise me if they all fell behind and, if we encounter severe weather, some may be lost."

"Very well, Captain, I suggest that you and I and the three captains go to see the governor at once and lay the matter before him."

Barely an hour later, Merriman, Egerton and the three captains were in the Governor's office together with a hastily summoned Goldberg. Governor Duncan opened the proceedings. "Captain Egerton, what is this all about, sir?"

"Sir, I think Captain Merriman could explain better than I can, but I will support him in all he has to say - Captain?"

"Thank you, sir. Now Governor, I will be direct, some of those transport ships are unsafe to travel in. They have no stores for a long voyage and are in poor condition. I think they should not be part of the convoy as they might endanger the other ships and men. They are likely to fall behind and will have to be abandoned. Certainly I would not wish to sail in such ill-found vessels or risk men's lives because of profit." Merriman looked round the group and said forcefully, "These three ships are all owned by Mr Goldberg, who will not spend the money necessary."

Goldberg leapt to his feet, shouting, "Rot and rubbish, sir, how dare you? They are as good as any other, my captains will tell you. Governor, how can you let this man talk like this?" Goldberg was going redder and redder in the face. "He is insulting me, sir, and I demand satisfaction."

"Sit down, Mr Goldberg, sit down I say. There will be no duels fought over this matter. Have you ever fought a duel? No, I thought not and you would most likely die if you did. Captain Merriman is an experienced naval officer and well able to face you with either pistol or sword. I have no doubt what the outcome would be."

Goldberg sat down, his florid face draining white as he realised what his hasty words had nearly got him into.

Merriman spoke quietly but all present were silent as they listened. "Gentlemen, I propose that a party of my very experienced boatswain and his mates, experienced seamen and one of my own officers, together with sail makers and one of Captain Egerton's officers inspect all three of Mr Goldberg's ships and report back to us their findings. How say you?"

All were in agreement except for a reluctant Goldberg. He said "Governor, why should this man tell us what to spend on our ships? He is an interloper and knows nothing of conditions here. Cordage, canvas and fittings are damnably expensive and I for one don't want his men poking about my ships. I forbid it."

"Forbid it all you like, Mr Goldberg, it will be done by my authority as Governor here in Bombay. I fully agree with Captain Merriman's proposals and if any ship is found to be unseaworthy and unlikely to survive the voyage it will be prevented from sailing."

"Damn you all. It's blackmail, that's what it is and I shall write a full report to the Company Head Office in London, of that you may be sure," shouted Goldberg in a rage as he stamped out of the room.

"Don't worry, gentlemen, I know that he is too mean to pay anything but his insurance on his ships, in fact I wouldn't be surprised if he was hoping for one or more to be lost so that he could claim for them."

"That's very true, sir," said one of the Goldberg captains. "He buys only cheap rubbish for a cargo. He stands to make more out of insurance than his trading."

The Governor nodded. "Captain Merriman, I thank you for bringing this situation to us all. Please carry on at once and have your people be very thorough."

Outside, Goldberg's three captains crowded round to thank Merriman. "You may have saved our lives, Captain. If any ship doesn't sail we will be out of work but we are all good seamen and some other trading company may employ us. Goldberg has brought this upon himself and I for one won't be sorry to see him losing money."

Back aboard *Lord Stevenage,* Merriman immediately ordered Lieutenant Weston to gather the men needed and proceed with the inspection of Goldberg's ships. He watched the boat pulling strongly for the frigate *Bombay* where they proceeded to take off Captain Egerton and another officer then headed for the suspect ships. Merriman watched this scene unfold before going to his cabin to shelter from the sun.

In the great cabin he found Grahame and Gupta in close conversation. Grahame looked up and said, "Ah, James, you are off with the convoy tomorrow, I believe, but I shall not be sailing with you. As you know, I have spent a lot of time these last few days questioning our prisoner Dumont and I have now collected much useful information. Our friend Gupta also has told me much of interest. Dumont has told me a lot about the pirates and indicated where he thinks Tipu's main shipyards are. I have made a list of them for you to investigate. We have to discover as much as we can about the fleet Tipu is building."

Merriman nodded and Grahame went on, "Now, James, there is another part of our problems. Dumont has confirmed that Den Bosch, the pirate leader, has spies here in Bombay, within the Company ranks. Uncovering that has to be my part in this matter but I am used to that sort of thing, as you well know, so that is why I shall not be sailing with you. Gupta here has come up with a cunning plan to find out more with which I am in full agreement."

"This is excellent news, sir. When I have assisted the Company Marine with the convoy, I'll come back as soon as possible to investigate those places on this list. What is this new plan that you have devised?"

"A bit of spying of our own, James. Is there an officer amongst your crew or the other ships who is of a dark hair and skin and could pass as a native?"

"I'm sure we could find one, sir, but what would he have to do?"

Grahame smiled. "A little play acting would be called for. The officer would have to go dressed like a beggar or a servant and our friend Gupta will go with him to translate and keep him safe in his role. Dark hair and dark eyes and dark-coloured skin should see him through."

"My God, sir, it's an awful risk. If he is discovered it will be almost certain death for the two of them. What about you, Gupta, are you sure that you want to do this?"

"Yes, sahib, I am sure. Tipu and French are enemies of us all and I want to help best I can. See, Merriman sahib, I have brought used and dirty Indian clothes for officer." He sniffed at them and said with a grimace, "Smell like beggar too."

"Don't worry, James, we must speak to the suitable men before we pick one and explain what he will have to do, but, he must be a volunteer, not just ordered to do it. I am used to travelling in disguise, and I know that with care he would be able to look like a native. I'm certain Gupta will look after him. Could one of the Company sloops be used to take them well down the coast with a small native boat and two or three trustworthy and reliable Indian crewmen from the Company's ships to sail it? They could get to one or two of the shipyards Dumont has told us about. It would be the quickest way, better than walking all that way or using a bullock cart. If a suitable man can be found they must go as soon as possible, in the dark of course. Normally I would go but I feel that I would be more use back here in Bombay."

In the event no suitable officer could be found in the Company vessels but *Lord Stevenage's* new lieutenant, Henry Merryweather was selected. He had volunteered as soon as he knew what was expected of him and indeed his very dark skin and hair and brown eyes made him ideal for the task.

Merriman spoke to him, saying, "Well, Lieutenant, I wish you the best of good fortune. If you are going to find where these ships are being built I will need to know as much as possible about any land defences they may have. But I insist that you make arrangements with the sloop's captain as to where you can be left and importantly where you can be picked up again."

Soon afterwards, Lieutenant Weston and his party returned to report his findings. "Of the three ships we inspected, sir, we found one to be utterly un-seaworthy. It is rotten and likely to break up in anything of a storm. Captain Egerton ordered it to be abandoned. The other two will need plenty of work to ropes and rigging which is being done now, sir, but they should be ready tomorrow. Captain Egerton demanded more rope, canvas and spare spars from Mr Goldberg's stores, of which there were plenty in spite of what he said, and he had all the crew of the abandoned ship divided up between the other two which did not have enough men to handle them safely and work the guns as well. Oh, and full supplies of stores and water are being supplied even now, sir."

"Excellent, Mr Weston, thank you. We may have to delay sailing in the morning until those ships are ready."

"One more thing, sir, that man Greely, well, we found his body floating in the harbour this morning. He was naked and his throat had been cut and the fish had been at him. We left him there, sir, his body will float out to sea. I hope I did right, sir."

"Yes, Lieutenant, I think you did. He was marked down as having run so he is no longer my responsibility. We are well rid of him."

That night, Merryweather and Gupta climbed down into a ship's boat with three native seamen from the frigate *Bombay*. With Midshipman Hungerford in command and half a dozen seamen at the oars, they were taken to the sloop *Villain* where a small fishing dhow had been made ready for them, well-provisioned for many weeks. As they left the frigate, Lieutenant Andrews sniffed loudly and said, "I think that Mr Merryweather will be alright, sir. He even smells like a beggar."

"That's right, David. I must have all the doors and windows opened to clear that foul air in my cabin."

Chapter Sixteen

The convoy sails

The convoy set sail the following day, a little later than Merriman had hoped but with a good wind behind it so he was optimistic progress should be made. The biggest difficulty had been to get the ships into the three lines. Eventually they were sorted out, with the accompaniment of much swearing, bellowing and furious arm waving from the escort ships, and the convoy moved on. The two frigates took positions on the leeward and landward side, the two Indiamen which looked like frigates on the starboard side, and a brig astern to chivvy up any stragglers and to keep a watch astern for any strange sail. The sloop ranged far ahead to be able to give warning of any impending attack.

Merriman left the deck to the duty watch and stumbled below, his shirt sticking to him with sweat and his stomach growling for the food Peters had ready for him. He had finished eating and was dressed in clean, dry clothes when he heard the marine outside thump his musket on the deck and announce, "First Lieutenant, sir."

"Come in, David. Is all well with our charges?"

"Generally speaking, sir, yes, but some of these merchant captains seem to have no idea what a straight line is. They keep wandering off station and have to be chased back."

Merriman thought about it for a few minutes then said, "Nothing unusual about that is there? You will remember the difficulties we had with convoys up and down the east coast of America, I'm sure. Independent and bull-headed characters the captains were, wanting to sail at their own speed and rules, spread out all over the sea. But they quickly saw sense at the first sight of a privateer or heard the first cannon shot. Then they came running back to the convoy like young chickens to the mother hen. We shall have to see what state the convoy is in by the morning. If you would make sure that all ships are showing stern lights for their fellows to follow, I would be obliged, but ensure that I am alerted if there is any trouble."

"Aye-Aye, sir, but I wouldn't be surprised if we have lost one or two by morning."

He left the cabin and Merriman wearily kicked off his shoes, rested his head on his arms on his desk and promptly fell asleep.

The following morning, at the faint first light of dawn, Merriman was on deck before his breakfast to see what condition the convoy was in. In the growing light he could see that several ships were out of line and all scattered over a wide area. Astern, the brig was endeavouring to make stragglers catch up. He was disgusted to see that many of them had shortened sail in the night against his orders, even though the sea conditions were ideal and with a good steady wind. *Damn convoys. If their masters can't sail better than that I will have no choice but to leave them behind. Blast them all, don't they want to be safe?*

Indeed two of the convoy were so far out of place that they must have passed between the two Indiamen on the starboard side to get to where they were. The leading Indiaman was far ahead of its position which in turn suggested that the lookouts and watch keepers were lax on that ship.

"Mr Andrews, general signal, all ships to close up immediately."

Merriman looked at the small midshipman of the watch, Mr Green, who was bending over the signal book whilst dragging flags out of the locker. "Mr Green, be careful you fly the correct signal flags, we don't want any accidents."

"Y-y- Yes, sir. I mean Aye-Aye, sir," said the boy, nervous at the thought of offending his captain. "Aye-aye, sir."

When the flags broke out aloft, some of the ships made an effort to close up into their allotted position but others seemed to ignore the signal and did not adjust their course. Merriman decided that he would have to show the awkward captains that he meant business.

He turned to the Sailing Master who had just appeared on deck. "Mr Cuthbert, it's as bad as I expected. We'll have to wake these captains up. Shorten sail if you please until we drop behind and then cross over to the starboard side of the convoy and close with those two ships outside the escort."

The frigate, with its greater speed, was soon in position close alongside one of the merchant ships.

"Get back in line, Captain, unless you want to make it easy for a privateer to take you," Merriman shouted into a speaking trumpet.

The reply when it came was short and to the point. "Bugger off. I'll not be told what to do by the bloody navy."

"If you don't, Captain I will be forced to board you and put one of my officers in command."

"Sheer off, you poncy navy bastard. I'll do as I like. You'll not board me," shouted the red-faced captain.

Merriman took a deep breath. "Mr Cuthbert, I would be obliged if you would gradually close with that ship, slowly, to give time for a boarding party to be gathered on deck."

The men were quickly ready with weapons clearly visible and with Lieutenant Shrigley at the head.

"Closer and closer if you will, Mr Cuthbert. I will try to force him to move over."

As the big frigate moved closer and closer to the other vessel, the captain hurled a stream of invective at Merriman, "Keep away, you stupid bugger. I'll see that the admiralty know about this treatment of an honest trader…"

Merriman ignored the man as his ship approached the other. The boarding party was obviously prepared to board and, when the other captain realised the futility of his position, he veered away. The frigate followed until the ship was back in its position with its captain swearing and waving his arms like a madman.

Merriman ignored him. "Mr Cuthbert, the same again with that other ship if you will, and we'll see what will happen."

In the event there was no need to do the same. The captain had seen what was happening and hastily changed course to regain the correct place in the convoy.

"Very good. Mr Cuthbert, place us close to that leading Indiaman please."

The officers on the quarterdeck of the Indiaman also had seen what had happened and reduced sail to allow the convoy to catch up. As the *Lord Stevenage* drew abreast, Merriman shouted across, "Please keep station better, Captain. I don't want to lose any of the sheep."

The reply was very different this time. "Aye-aye, Captain. Our fault, difficult to get used to sailing so slowly, don't you know."

Merriman waved in answer. "Very good, Captain, and thank you."

Whilst all that was happening, the rest of the convoy, chivvied by the other escorts, had managed to assemble in something like their right order. Happily the weather continued fair and with a good sailing wind under their coat-tails the ships made good progress all day. As evening approached with its usual rapidity, Merriman began to hope that the various captains had learned their lesson and would manage to keep more or less in the right place overnight.

The third and fourth days continued without incident. The usual shipboard work and exercises by the gun crews and the marines were continued but Merriman thought their luck was too good to last.

Chapter Seventeen

Pirate fleet attacks

Weeks passed and, with good weather and strong winds, nothing untoward happened until the convoy was off the Maldive Islands. Merriman and Mr Cuthbert had ensured, by careful navigation, that no land had been sighted since leaving Bombay. Several small native craft had been seen, fishing boats and small traders which rapidly made off towards the Islands.

Merriman, standing on the quarterdeck with the officer of the watch, Mr Shrigley, turned to the Master who was trying to teach navigation to the midshipmen.

"Mr Cuthbert, it would not surprise me if those fishermen told some of the pirates there where we are and what our course is, so I think it would be wise to alter course three degrees to starboard to give them further to go. Mr Shrigley, I'll have a signal made to the convoy accordingly."

He turned to watch Midshipman Small drag the flags out of the locker but realised that he had been standing for too long in one spot. His shoes were stuck to the tarred caulking between the deck boards which had softened in the heat. With an effort he pulled them free, laughing at his own stupidity.

Surprisingly the convoy managed to turn onto the new course fairly well with the exception of the ship which had given them trouble before. That one was slow to obey, obviously the captain trying to show his independence. *Blast the man, he just wants to be awkward,* Merriman mused. "Mr Small, signal that ship to keep better station, he is a damned nuisance. No not that last bit, Mr Small."

The course change did not work and a group of dhows was sighted astern the following day at dawn. A drowsy Merriman was fully awakened by his servant Peters standing by his cot.

"Sorry to wake you, sir, but some dhows have been sighted. Midshipman Green was sent down to wake you, sir."

That brought Merriman out of the cot and he was struggling to get fully dressed with Peters' help when the thud of the marine sentry's musket on the deck and his call, "First Lieutenant, sir," brought him out into the great cabin.

"Enter," he called and Andrews appeared.

"There is a mixed collection of dhows following us, sir, one of them is bigger than the one we sank before and they are obviously trying to catch us, sir."

Once on deck, Merriman could see the ships clearly. There were fourteen of them with their sails shining almost golden in the light from the sun low on the eastern horizon.

"Mr Andrews, beat to quarters and clear for action. Make a general signal to all ships, Enemy in sight. Close up and prepare for action. Fire a gun to get their attention, a signal to the escorts. Fall back to positions as agreed."

Whilst the hustle and bustle went on around him, Merriman tried to watch all ships at once. Incredibly the merchant vessels were doing what they had been told, moving closer together to leave less sea area to be defended. Merriman was pleased to see that even the awkward ship was one of the first to obey. The pirate ships, and there was no doubt that they were pirates for the red flags flew above them all, were closing rapidly and spreading out into a line some nine abreast, which was what Egerton had told him they would do. The largest of the pirate ships had placed itself in the centre of the line but slightly ahead with other smaller ships on the flanks and the rest following. It took Merriman no more than two or three seconds to decide on his tactics and he called his officers to him.

"Gentlemen, the biggest of those ships is the first one we must deal with. She appears to have some big guns, maybe eighteen pounders, which would cause havoc if it got into the convoy. This is what I propose. We will go about and steer towards the biggest ship and pass her to starboard with all starboard guns to fire as they bear. Then a broadside on the one to larboard. All guns loaded with solid shot and fired at the waterline. Then we'll be in reach of two more of the smallest ships and give them a broadside each before we turn back to the biggest one and pass her stern to give it another full broadside.

If all goes well that should finish them as fighting ships and we will go after the rest. Some will get past us but we must rely on the Indiamen and the brig and the other frigate to hold them until we can get back to help. To your stations, gentlemen, and I want the ship to go about like lightning when the time comes."

On the quarter deck Merriman was accompanied by Lieutenant Andrews and the midshipmen, Hungerford, at his station by the signal locker. Small and Green were ready to run with messages. Mr Cuthbert was with four men at the wheel and the marines lined up on either side behind the hammock nettings with their muskets ready. Captain St James and Lieutenant Goodwin and their sergeants were striding up and down behind them.

"There's an awful lot of them, sir, can we beat them?" said a white-faced and trembling Midshipman Green.

Merriman smiled down at him. "We can deal with them, Edward. Stay by me and remember what your duty is."

Poor Green was so amazed at the Captain calling him by given name that his worries about pirates receded for a while.

"Stand by to go about," yelled Merriman. "Gun deck be ready ... right, Mr Cuthbert, hard over."

The men on the big wheel spun it with all their strength while the sail handlers hauled madly at the sheets, braces and bowlines to bring the ship back under control and charging back diagonally at the enemy line.

It seemed only a moment before the *Lord Stevenage* was passing across the pirate flotilla and turning between the big dhow and another on its starboard side. Immediately both dhows fired their guns as the frigate passed between them but the guns were badly aimed and some did not fire at all. Nevertheless, Merriman felt the thuds as shot hit the side of the *Lord Stevenage* and wood splinters flew from the bulwarks. On the gun deck, one gun was overturned with men trapped beneath it screaming for help. At the same time, the frigate's guns began to fire, Lieutenants Weston and Shrigley running back along the deck to ensure that no gun fired before the target appeared in front of it.

"Reload, men, reload" yelled Weston, choking and coughing on the powder smoke as it swirled about him.

"Mr Cuthbert, bring her round across her stern," yelled Merriman.

The helm went over and the ship began to turn rapidly as the crew hauled madly on the ropes controlling the sails. The constant gun drill now proved its worth as, by the time the ship passed the big dhow's stern, Shrigley's guns were ready and Weston's only a minute later. Merriman had sent young Mr Green down to the gun deck with a message for Lieutenant Weston, "The Captain's complements, sir, and will you fire as your guns bear."

The guns roared out one by one, the heavy shot bursting through the stern of the dhow and killing scores of the pirates.

"Mr Cuthbert, we'll pass as close as we can behind the next two small ones and give them a broadside each before we go about to give the big one another broadside."

The big dhow shuddered as the shot went home and there was little cannon fire in return although many pirates were shooting badly aimed muskets. Some of the shots were effective as one of the marines fell back with blood pouring from a hole in his forehead and one of the men at the big wheel was lying in a crumpled heap on the deck.

Looking back, Merriman saw that he need not worry about either of the first two ships. Both were listing as water poured into them through shot holes on the water line and both of them had lost masts. Screaming pirates were falling or jumping overboard. The other two small dhows were sinking slowly, also finished.

"Now, Mr Cuthbert, have the reefs out of the tops'ls and steer for the ships ahead. Try to pass between two of them if you can. We should be able to catch them."

The orders were quickly passed and the Topmen going aloft like monkeys. With the extra canvas the ship immediately increased speed.

Two of the dhows had passed their sinking comrades and were making for rear of the convoy where the Indiamen were waiting for them. Other pirates had all sailed nearer to the larboard side of the convoy whilst Merriman was dealing with the first four and the frigate *Bombay* and the small brig *Hannah* had turned to meet them. The *Lord Stevenage* was now on her best point of sailing and was catching up rapidly.

"Mr Shrigley, go for'ard and see what you can do with the bow chasers. The crews are waiting for orders."

"Aye-aye, sir" replied the Lieutenant, quickly climbing up to the fo'c'sle where the two big guns were pointing ahead. Almost instantly they both fired, one shot went well off target but the other ball struck a dhow full on the stern and crashed through the length of it, killing or wounding many of the men aboard.

"Well done. Again if you please, Mr Shrigley," shouted Merriman.

Both guns were ready in moments and two more cannonballs sent on their way. This time the aim was better, one shot again hit the same dhow on the stern which completely shattered its rudder. The other struck a second dhow, inflicting damage which caused it to turn away as its mast folded in the middle and crashed down onto the men beneath.

As *Lord Stevenage* surged past them, carronades on either side of the fo'c'sle fired, a hail of musket balls sweeping aside the crowd of men on the decks of the dhows. The marines were firing as rapidly as they could, picking off the men up in the rigging, blood pouring down the sides of the ships in crimson streams. Those ships were finished as a threat but what of the rest? Continuous gunfire could be heard but the gun smoke ahead prevented clear vision.

"Aloft with you, Mr Hungerford, tell me what is happening," shouted Merriman.

Hungerford climbed like a monkey up a tree and surveyed the action ahead. "One more of the enemy is sinking, sir. *Bombay* is engaging another two and one has managed to get alongside *Hannah* to board her. I think the Indiamen have dealt with the other two that passed us, sir, but three others are nearly up to the convoy."

"Very good, Mr Hungerford, come down now. Mr Cuthbert, I'll have the courses reset, we must catch those three and if we can help the brig with a few shots into her attacker as we go past, so much the better. Captain St James, have all your men ready to fire into the pirate when they can. Mr Green, my compliments to Mr Weston and ask him to fire some shots into the pirate's waterline."

The crew of the brig was fighting desperately to hold back the flood of boarders but were fast losing ground. Somebody on the pirate dhow saw the big frigate approaching and screamed a warning to his fellows. Panic ensued, half the pirates on the brig wanted to carry on fighting, the others desperately tried to get back to their own ship, but too late. Three of the frigate's cannon exploded as one, the balls ripping into the dhow right on the waterline. The marines were again shooting as fast as they could reload, causing havoc among the pirates and, with the sudden help given to them, the brig's defenders were able to deal with the pirates left aboard and cut the ropes used by the pirates to tie the two ships together. A loud cheer rang out as *Lord Stevenage* passed and an officer on the quarterdeck waved his hat wildly. Merriman raised his in acknowledgement.

Now for the other three, he thought grimly. "Mr Shrigley, try the bow chasers again but be careful not to hit a merchant ship."

Both fired with no visible effect but the dhows had slowed down to attack the slower merchantmen and the frigate, travelling like the wind, was nearly up with them. The pirates scattered but too late, the frigate caught up and, passing between two of them, unleashed both larboard and starboard broadsides. The two unfortunate vessels seemed to disintegrate but the third managed to turn to larboard and before the frigate could fire again or even attempt to turn, it was away, too fast to be caught.

"Mr Cuthbert, take her round and we'll go back and see how the other ships are faring."

"Aye-aye, sir," replied the old sailing master with a big grin on his face, before bawling the necessary orders.

"We'll show those other ships how good a King's ship really is."

Lord Stevenage seemed to spin round on the spot before heading back towards the *Bombay* and the *Hannah*. All gunfire had ceased and both ships appeared to be only slightly damaged. Merriman rubbed his hands together with delight.

"Mr Hungerford, signal for both the captains to heave to and report to me. Then signal to the Indiamen the same. Mr Andrews, clear from action stations and have my cabin put back at once."

Both Captain Egerton and Captain Oliver arrived almost together, Oliver with a bloody bandage wrapped round his head. Both were bursting with excitement as the strain of battle was over, both wanting to shake Merriman by the hand and congratulate him on the success of his planning. The captains of the Indiamen, having further for their boats to row, soon arrived and joined in the congratulations.

Merriman, not a little embarrassed by the praise heaped upon him, suggested that they all went below. "My cabin should be back to rights now, gentlemen, and I think we all deserve a drink."

The cabin was indeed ready, with Peters and Tomkins bringing up the last of the furniture and other items from below. Peters, the ever attentive and thoughtful servant, had already brought wine and glasses up and he and Tomkins immediately began to dispense it to all the officers.

"A toast, gentlemen, to the damnation of all pirates!"

That toast drunk with great enthusiasm, Merriman asked for reports on damage and losses.

"Mr Oliver, I'll start with you as your ship was the only one the pirates boarded. Apart from yourself how many men of your crew have been wounded and how many dead are there?"

The jollity disappeared from Oliver's face as he reported, "Little damage to my ship, sir, the attackers had only one cannon which they couldn't use properly. Their principal mode of attack was to overwhelm the victim with boarders. My guns inflicted a lot of damage before they got alongside. The crew fought well, sir, but we were nearly beaten when your ship appeared. We lost eight men dead and fifteen wounded, some of whom may not live. We don't have a proper doctor aboard to tend them so we will lose more," he finished gloomily.

"Thank you, Captain, a very clear account. I have a very good surgeon aboard; I will send him over to you. Your written report should go to Captain Egerton but I would like to have a copy. Now then, Captain, how did it go with you?"

"Well, sir, we sank one of them very quickly and were engaged with two more when you passed but we left both of them floating, burning wrecks. I have three dead and only six wounded. Those were due to badly aimed musket fire, sir."

"And how did your ships manage, Captains?" said Merriman, turning to the captains of the Indiamen.

Both laughed and one replied, "No real trouble at all, sir, there were two of them but as you had suggested we had all our cannon direct their fire at the waterline. Between us we sank them both. We didn't rescue any of them, sir," he added significantly. "Between us we lost only five men to musket fire."

"Excellent, gentlemen. By my count the pirates have lost thirteen of the fourteen ships they started with and only one escaped. They must have lost hundreds of men. We have taught them a hard lesson which I hope will stop them raiding more Company convoys, for some time at least."

"Our success is largely due to your careful planning ahead, sir, and for insisting that all of us knew what to do when the time came," said Captain Egerton. "Your ship handling was wonderful, sir, and you destroyed four of them in as many minutes. I saw it before gun smoke obscured my view and we were in action ourselves."

"Thank you, sir, but we all did well. I think you should all return to your commands now, gentlemen, but I should like to entertain you to dinner here tomorrow evening. Meanwhile the convoy will continue on course."

Chapter Eighteen

Escort leaves convoy

The next evening, the men enjoyed a convivial dinner of roast chicken and such vegetables as were still available. That was followed by a new dessert, an Indian concoction prepared as a result of Peters and the cook visiting the Governor's kitchen as he had suggested, and all captains were full and feeling happy with their world. The company including Lieutenant Anderson, captain of the sloop *Clive* which had been sailing far ahead of the convoy. Anderson had heard the gunfire but arrived back too late to help. Lieutenants David Andrews and Alfred Shrigley and the ship's three midshipmen were there also, the midshipmen filling themselves with food as fast as they could.

"Upon my word, Alfred," said Merriman, "I think you have a new contender for the eating title that you had when you were a midshipman. Mr Small seems to exceed even your capacity. Now, Mr Green, if you can leave that chicken leg alone for long enough, I believe it is for you to propose the Loyal Toast."

"Y-y-yes, sir," squeaked the boy, fumbling for his glass. "The King, gentlemen."

As the time had not yet come when a king had decreed that the navy could drink his toast sitting down, all stood and raised their glass, the taller ones standing awkwardly with bent heads beneath the deckhead.

When all were settled, Merriman cleared his throat and said, "I think the time has come when we shall have to part company, gentlemen. The convoy is now past the worst piracy area and, keeping well to the east of Madagascar, you should have no more trouble. If you two Indiamen can stay with the convoy at least until it reaches the Cape, your appearance as well-armed frigates would have the desired effect. After that it should then be safe."

"Why must we part now, sir?" asked one of the Indiaman captains.

"Because I have an even more urgent matter to attend to, sir." Merriman told them all about the Napoleonic threat to India and the possibility of Tipu building a fleet. "So you see, there is more that I must do to find out what I can of that matter, and do what I can to disrupt any shipbuilding."

Of course the officers of the marine knew all about it but neither of the two captains of the Indiamen did and they were shocked at the news.

And so it was arranged for the following day. The convoy hove to while boats rowed busily between them. All captains of the convoy were told why the escort was leaving them and, apart from a few grumbles, they accepted it. The afternoon found the two frigates, the sloop and the brig on their way back to Bombay with at least fourteen days sailing to get there. Merriman was relieved of the responsibility of the convoy but he was still desperately worried about Merryweather and Gupta on their spying expedition.

Chapter Nineteen

Discoveries by British Agents

The two beggars shambling along near the harbour of Mangalore seemed little different from the scores of other people making their way along the road. The only thing which made them stand out was that the smaller man was pulling the bigger man along by a rope tied round his waist. That man was walking with his head down, occasionally waving his arms about and, when his face was seen, it was like that of an imbecile, with staring eyes and open mouth from which strings of saliva ran down his chin and dripped onto his filthy shirt. He appeared to be dumb and could only make strange grunting noises.

Merryweather, for he was the bigger man, was finding it difficult to keep up the pretence but sheer willpower drove him on. In truth he was regretting the decision that he should be disguised as a beggar. He was dirty, smelly and pestered by lice and he hated it. The smaller man, Gupta, told anybody who asked that he had promised his mother to take the man, his uncle, his father's brother, to other members of his family. Gupta's father had died and his mother couldn't cope with the imbecile anymore. That story had served them well over the days when they were ashore. They begged for food and shelter when they could and slept in the occasional barn whose owner took pity on them. Sometimes they slept outdoors well away from the road.

Things had gone well for them after being dropped in the night into the small dhow which the East India Marine sloop had brought with them. They had sailed along the coast looking into many of the rivers and bays they could see, finding large shipbuilding activity at only one place by the name of Bhatkal, which they took a note of. There seemed to be no forts to defend the harbour. Knowing that they were approaching Mangalore they decided to go on foot along the north side of the river having arranged with the three Company seamen to pick them up at the south side of the river mouth in four days. Suitable signals were settled upon.

"My God, Gupta, I don't know how long this will take, but the lice have made themselves quite at home in my hair and clothing. Damn the little blighters." Merryweather emphasised his words with vigorous scratching.

They had stopped for the night in a small clearing away from the road and Merryweather took the opportunity to strip off his clothing. He occupied himself searching for the lice and their eggs in the seams then popping them between his fingers.

"The next water we find, Gupta, I must try to wash myself."

They spoke in whispers in case any other ears were near and Gupta replied, "Yes, Uncle, I will try and buy some soap in the next village."

So far they had observed several tiny villages up small rivers but seen no sign of large shipbuilding other than at Bhatkal. They were more hopeful that Mangalore would show them what they had come so far to find. Mangalore town was well inland and connected to the sea by a long, wide river which wound southwards for many miles before reaching the sea. Gupta said that he had been there as a slave on the pirate dhow and had seen big ships being built and a big fort on the other side of the river.

They were put ashore on a deserted beach and began walking inland to find the river. As the eastern sky began to lighten they found a place to stop where they could sleep, hopefully without being seen, before going on to the river. Refreshed, they continued, up and over small hills, until the river came in sight. They looked down on a huge shipbuilding site with three big ships under construction and three others, frigates by the size of them, moored together on the other side of the river stern on to a huge masonry wall and almost complete by the look of them. Some men could be seen on the decks and other men were carrying timber and fitments aboard.

Fortunately their disguise as beggars was good because, having seen the activity for only a few minutes, they were accosted by three men, heavily bearded and wearing red turbans.

They were soldiers or guards carrying long muskets and each with a sword thrust through his sash.

"Clear off, you two. Take your stinking selves away from here. Who are you anyway?"

Gupta related their cover story whilst Merryweather continued to look as stupid and idiotic as possible on the end of his rope.

The three guards carefully kept themselves to windward as the leader said, "You are on the wrong side of the river if you are going south. You'll have to go a long way upstream before you can cross over. Now, be off with you."

Gupta hopefully thrust out his hand, palm up. "Have pity, soldier sahib, we need to buy food."

"You'll get nothing from us," said the man, thumping Gupta on the chest with the butt of his musket. "Clear off I say, and take your filthy idiot uncle with you."

They watched for a while whilst Gupta and Merryweather shambled off along the north side of the river.

"Your disguise was good enough to fool those three, Uncle. Even I could be fooled. Anyway, we have seen what we needed to see but we still have to cross the river to find the coast again."

They shambled on, eventually coming to a village with a small temple where they were taken pity on by a monk and given some rice and water before being sent away.

Two days later, as darkness fell with its tropical rapidity, they came to a point where the river narrowed and they decided to try and cross to go south on the other side. Merryweather, with sundry grunts and arm waving pointed to a small boat tied up nearby which could suit their purpose. Therefore, later that night they stole quietly down to the water's edge, untied the boat, and set off for the other side. They had misjudged the force of the current though and the boat was borne quickly downstream. As dawn broke, they passed a huge fort overlooking the river.

"That is Sultan fort, sahib, big fort, many guns," said Gupta.

"Well, Gupta, at least we know where it is. We are going in the right direction, it will save a lot of walking, but we must try to row across at some point."

Their prayers were answered and the current split round a sandbar. They found themselves in slack water on the south side of the river. Quickly they waded ashore with Merryweather taking the opportunity to immerse himself in the hope of washing himself a bit, but it only served to rouse the lice to further activity.

They set off again with Merryweather still in his role of an idiot and Gupta pulling him along on the rope. They begged for food in every village they passed through, with success more often not, until on the late afternoon of the fourth day they realised that they were somewhere near a ruined temple behind the beach where they expected to be picked up. Gupta left Merryweather hidden behind the temple while he set off in the dark with the small lantern he had managed to keep hidden in his rags.

Doing his best to ensure that he could not be seen, he flashed the pre-arranged signal out to sea but there was no answering flash of light. He waited for half an hour and tried once more but again no reply. By now he was getting worried but he persevered until finally, after several hours, he saw the answering flash from the dhow, closer inshore than he expected. He turned to fetch his companion but found him close by.

"I couldn't sleep, Gupta, so I watched with you."

Only a few moments later the small dhow appeared through the gloom and anchored. The two men thankfully waded out to it and climbed aboard, exhausted, and the three seamen promptly raised the sail and headed out to sea.

After a quick bite to eat and a very welcome drink, followed by an attempt to clean up and change into clean clothes, Merryweather ordered them to sail back to Bombay, keeping a watch out for the sloop that had set them off on their journey. Then he and Gupta crawled under a spare sail and a pile of nets and were soon asleep.

Chapter Twenty

Pirate leader desperate

The Dutchman, Den Bosch, was restless and worried, although one wouldn't know it to look at him. He leant back in a reclining chair with his feet up on a stool, holding a glass of punch in one hand and a cigar in the other. He was alone except for the servant squatting in the corner of the veranda waiting patiently and silently for his next order. The view from the veranda was magnificent, blue sky and blue sea breaking on the golden sandy beach where native fishermen were mending their nets and working on their boats. With a gentle breeze off the sea to keep him cool, what else could be needed for a tropical paradise? Women maybe, but he was not attracted to any of those he came across.

In spite of all that, the Dutchman was restless. In his bungalow in a native village by a small inlet in the north of the Maldive Islands, he was more unsettled than ever. He had heard of the loss of so many of his pirate ships in the two attacks on his ships on the Malabar Coast. *It must be that new Royal Navy frigate that has put some backbone into the Company ships. Curse it, I must find out more about it.*

The Dutchman had his own sources of information, provided by some disaffected coolies or clerks in the East India Company's offices, even one senior man. He also had agents in several of the small villages and harbours and trading posts along the coast. He had moved further north from the Seychelles, and then on to the Maldives to the small harbour where his ships now lay, but it had been a long time since anything was reported. Then word had arrived that the British warship had appeared.

As usual he had his dhows out looking for prey, but they had found nothing for weeks and the crews were becoming bored. And now the damned Frenchman, Dumont, had been lost with two ships of his squadron. Following the losses in the previous weeks, it was too much. The surviving two ships had reported that, when a ship had been seen, they had moved in to attack but realised too late that it was a frigate ready for action and Dumont had been lost.

Den Bosch had also heard nothing from his man in Bombay, which was strange. He had been told that the Company was gathering a convoy together to sail in the next few days but nothing more. Eventually he had received warning from fishermen that the convoy was passing the Maldives and he sent fourteen dhows after it, expecting rich pickings.

Now there was even worse news. A single ship had returned from the fourteen he had sent out after the convoy. All the captain could tell him was that they had been outclassed and beaten by four frigates and a brig guarding that convoy and none of his ships and men had survived. Until now Den Bosch had been the main pirate captain and had no difficulty in finding men to crew his dhows and other ships, but with news of these losses of both ships and men, his reputation had received a severe blow. He must do better next time or he was finished.

He resolved to send some of his men northward, even as far as Bombay, to offer his spies more money for worthwhile information or death if they failed to keep him informed. And, he wondered, would his small fleet be safe in the Maldives? The small dhows would be alright, passing themselves off as simple fishermen, but his frigate and the biggest dhows were too big to hide. All the islands were low lying with no hill or dunes rising more than eight or ten feet above the sea level, so concealment was impossible. The more he thought about it, he realised that the English ship and Company ships would probably come looking for him here. They would have realised that the attack had happened soon after they had passed the Maldives and his ships must have been waiting there.

Damn them all, he would have to move, but where? It must be further east, Ceylon perhaps, they wouldn't chase him that far, would they? No sooner had he decided than he gave orders to his captains to be ready to sail. The smallest of the dhows could be left behind to tell him what was happening.

Chapter Twenty-One

Next target surveyed

The *Lord Stevenage* and other ships were approaching the latitude of the southern coast of India when Merriman, taking his customary walk on the quarterdeck, suddenly stopped dead as a thought struck him. He froze for a moment, then continued walking, mulling over his new idea whilst tugging on his ear as was usual when deep in thought. The others on deck watched him, hardly daring to move for fear of interrupting his train of thought. They knew that their captain often came up with new ideas when walking.

Merriman turned to the officer of the watch. "Mr Shrigley, after we have all breakfasted, signal all ships to heave to and captains and first lieutenants to come aboard. When they get here I want all my officers to join them in my cabin."

"Aye-aye, sir," said Shrigley and then, greatly daring, added, "I think you must have thought of a good plan to show our teeth again to our enemies."

"Yes, Alfred, I hope I have. I'll tell you when we are all together."

He disappeared below and found Peters setting out his breakfast. It was a plain meal as all the fresh bread and vegetables had been finished, but he relished his black coffee and hard bread with some kind of Indian preserve spread on it. Once breakfast was over and the table cleared, he spread out the chart of the southern Malabar Coast showing many small inlets and rivers. The sailing master's charts and notes, with additions made by Captain Egerton, were surprisingly clear. He knew instantly what his orders would be. He continued to refine his plan and was deep in thought when the marine sentry banged his musket on the deck and announced, "Midshipman of the watch, sir."

It was Gideon Small who burst in and excitedly said, "Lieutenant Shrigley's compliments, sir, and the other captains are nearly here, sir, and will you come on deck?" He seemed to say all that in a gabble and without drawing breath.

"Thank you, Mr Small. Now make your report again, slower and more distinctly this time, and stand up straight when you do."

The red-faced and crestfallen midshipman replied, "Yes, sir, sorry, sir," before he repeated the message.

"Very well, Mr Small, back on deck with you. I'll be up directly."

Each of the three captains and their lieutenants were welcomed aboard with all the usual ceremony. Two lines of marines presented arms and Boatswain's whistles sounded clear and shrill. The first to appear over the side was Captain Egerton, raising his hat to Merriman and his officers who acknowledged him. When all had arrived, Merriman asked them down to the great cabin. His own officers followed except for Lieutenant Weston and the midshipman who were on watch.

"Please be seated, gentlemen, and remove your coats if you wish. It is too hot to stand on ceremony. Peters, serve the tea or coffee as each requires." Peters and Tomkins bustled about and finally disappeared. "Now then, gentlemen, I have been thinking again about the reason my ship is here. As I told you, we know that Tipu Sultan is building a fleet of warships in the hope of gaining control of the western coast but more importantly to help Napoleon and his army to reach India. That is the main reason, only secondly was I to help you deal with the pirates. On the way here my ship sank two pirate ships. Then in our first attack by Captain Anderson's sloop we burned three more and in our attack on the harbour at Karwar we destroyed perhaps another eight or ten. And only a few days ago we sank thirteen more making a total of around twenty six. I believe that we have dealt them a serious blow and their losses of men must have been enormous. Of course we haven't seen anything of the larger vessels they are reported to have, perhaps one or two brigs and even a frigate."

"Captain Merriman, sir, I agree that we have caused much trouble for the pirates but I don't think the problem has been completely dealt with," Edgerton replied. "It may take some time, but I expect that they will recruit more men and find some more ships. Many of the native people are living on the edge of poverty and piracy may seem to be the only way they can find to feed their families. As far as the pirates go, I believe they have at least one frigate hidden somewhere. Earlier this year, April I believe it was, a French frigate named *La Preneuse* and another ship brought volunteers, I understand some hundred and fifty of them, from Ile de France, Mauritius we call it, to join Tipu's army and help to train his men. *La Preneuse* left, leaving the other behind somewhere, but where we don't know."

"Maybe so, Captain," replied Merriman. "But you should be free of trouble for many weeks. Now I would like to tell you what I propose to do next. You will remember that we have a French prisoner aboard. Mr Cuthbert the master and Mr Grahame spent a long time questioning him and, under threat of the hangman's noose, he was quite forthcoming about other harbours which pirates use and which are big enough for shipbuilding. Two of them are on the southern coast of India. They are Chettuva and Beypore. Do any of you know them, gentleman?"

"I know where they are, Captain. Occasionally we have patrolled along most of the coast but being so few of us we haven't been able to inspect any of those southern harbours closely," said Captain Egerton to murmurs of agreement and chattering from the Marine officers.

Merriman cleared his throat loudly to get their attention and then said, "What I propose, gentlemen, is that we *do* investigate those harbours as closely as we can to see if we can find any warships being built and destroy them if so. If there are pirates there we will destroy them too." More excited chattering followed Merriman's comments until he raised his hand. "I know that it is not part of the duties of the Marine ships to go looking for Tipu's fleet but I would appreciate your help."

Egerton rose to his feet, looked round at the eager faces and said, "Captain Merriman, sir, since you arrived in Bombay we have seen more successful action than we have had in months, and you are to be thanked for that. I am convinced that the Company and the Governor would be only too pleased for us to do everything we can to help you. As the senior Marine officer I must say that I am prepared to put our ships entirely at your disposal, sir, and looking at the faces around me, I don't think we shall have any lack of volunteers for whatever you wish to do, sir."

There was more excitement and Egerton's First Lieutenant Wilde, calling for quiet, said, "Captain Merriman, I think I speak for all, sir, we are all eager for more action and look forward to hearing your plans for us."

"Thank you, gentlemen, I am most gratified by your comments. Mr Andrews, please be good enough to unroll our chart." That done and the chart held down by various items before it could roll itself up again, Merriman continued, "I believe that we are nearly opposite the place named Chettuva so we'll start with that. You remember the raid we carried out at Karwar when we sent in the sloop to put a small party ashore at night to observe any activity there may be? My chart shows that the harbour here is behind a long narrow headland. Is that correct, Captain?"

"Yes, sir, it is. I took my ship up the river there a long time ago and saw a small shipyard building little native craft. At that time the headland did not appear to very wide or very high, mostly sand dunes rising to a higher level at the end. I remember thinking that that would be an excellent position to construct a fort to defend the entrance if one were needed."

"Excellent. Then I propose that the sloop *Clive,* under Captain Johnson, creeps as close to the shore as possible in the dark and three of your men with an officer, land and attempt to see exactly what is behind that headland now. Our bigger ships will stay well offshore and out of sight. Mr Anderson, you must make sure that you recover your men and be out of sight of land before dawn. That is imperative. What we do next depends on what you find out. A lot rests on your report and on your shoulders. Any questions, gentlemen? No? Good, and remember that the unexpected always happens, as some writer put it."

So it was that the ships approached the land in the dark and hove-to. The sloop quietly crept inshore and anchored. A boat was lowered and the three men and Anderson's Lieutenant Jamieson slipped ashore. They soon reached the top of a ridge of sand dunes from where the harbour lay before them. A rough road was behind the harbour leading off towards the end of the headland. What had been described as a small boatyard was now much bigger and by the light of a few lanterns scattered about it, they could see a large ship under construction and piles of timber ready for use. Nobody seemed to be working but a few indistinct figures could be seen wandering about, probably guards.

Jamieson decided it would be too risky to try and get any closer. They now knew what was happening and Jamieson was about to order them to leave when one of his men nudged him and pointed up river. The silhouetted shape of a ship could only just be seen, obviously anchored and with no lights showing. A few moments later the lieutenant was certain it was no bigger than a frigate, but whether it was armed and ready for sea he could not see. Certainly no masts could be seen against the high land behind it and Jamieson decided they had seen enough. Then he remembered Captain Egerton's comments about a fort and decided they must investigate further.

It took only ten minutes or so to reach the end of the headland where they could see no sign of a fort, although they found piles of stone and timber, doubtless ready for some sort of construction, most probably a fort.

Dawn was barely showing when they reached the sloop and climbed back aboard. Anderson lost no time in heading off shore to find the other ships.

Chapter Twenty-Two

Shipyard attacked

"That is excellent news, Lieutenant," said Merriman when the report was passed on to him and the other officers gathered aboard *Lord Stevenage*. "Captain Egerton, when you sailed up the river there, sir, some time ago I believe you said, what would you say the average depth of water was?"

"At any state of the tide there should be enough water to allow our frigates in, sir, but I don't know if there are any new sandbars now. The river has not been sounded for a long time."

"Very well, gentlemen, I don't think it would be wise to risk our frigates in there but a smaller vessel could do so. From Lieutenant Jamieson's report I think we can do plenty of damage to the ships and shipyard and so this is what I propose to do tonight…"

That night, the sloop *Clive* crept up river to where the frigate was anchored. Fortunately the wind was blowing across the river and under reduced canvas the ship made slow progress until it was well past the anchored frigate where Captain Anderson judged the position was right. In whispers he then ordered the ship put about and they crept down river, near to the anchored frigate. Then he ordered the already prepared stern anchor to be let go, quietly, and all sails clewed up. The ship gently tugged at the anchor but he was pleased to see that the river's flow was not too strong for what he had to do.

Meanwhile, a party of sailors and marines from the *Lord Stevenage* landed on the beach of the headland with Merriman in the lead and Seaman Ted Jackson with him. Jackson had been a poacher before the press had swept him up and he had an uncanny ability to see in the dark. Merriman sent him ahead then waited with his men off the beach and in the sand dunes until Jackson came back.

"It's just like we were told, sir, not far ahead is a big dune and we can see the harbour from it."

"Good man, pass the word to advance, quietly now, until we are all in line as arranged, then we'll wait for the signal."

The seamen were burdened with several kegs of gunpowder, fuses and combustibles and Merriman checked that they knew exactly what they had to do. Lieutenant Weston and Midshipman Hayward passed the word and then they settled down to wait.

Aboard the sloop, Captain Anderson checked his watch for the umpteenth time then decided that enough time had elapsed for Merriman to get in position. He whispered to Lieutenant Clarkson to be ready with his party.

"All ready, Mr Clarkson, sir, we know what we are going to do. If you can put us close enough we can climb aboard with all we need. It should provide a grand explosion, sir."

Lieutenant Clarkson quietly issued the orders. "Right, men, let out that anchor cable slowly and quietly until we are alongside that ship, then you men with the ropes tie us to the chains."

Slowly they let the sloop drift quietly down to the frigate and, with hardly a bump, fetched up alongside. Anderson and his men rapidly boarded with their bundles and kegs of gunpowder and disappeared into the darkness. Ten minutes later they appeared again and quickly climbed aboard their own ship.

"All done, sir, there was only one man aboard, a guard perhaps, fast asleep. We saw to it that he won't wake up again. We put the explosives and the rest on the lower deck and against the side. I set the fuses for ten minutes, sir, so we should get away quickly. Oh, and that ship was only just built, sir, there were no partitions or fixings or guns aboard but I saw that all three lower masts had been stepped."

Anderson had already ordered the ties and the anchor cable cut and, to the muffled thud of an axe, the sloop was suddenly free with the Topmen racing aloft to set the topsails. The ship rapidly gathered way and under topsails and jibs was soon well away from the anchored frigate and round a bend in the river before the charges exploded.

That was the signal Merriman had been waiting for and he and his men surged forward, running down the dunes, over the road and into the shipyard. The few guards there were looking across the river to see what had happened. They stood no chance and were dealt with by the marines using their bayonets.

Without delay, the seamen piled the kegs and other combustible material against the stern and rudder and by the stem of the part-built warship, piling timber and anything burnable they could find on top. There was now plenty of light from the blazing frigate and Merriman ordered everyone back to the beach, waiting with the men delegated to set fire to the fuses. That done, they raced back into the dunes with the marines taking pot shots back to where the suddenly awoken villagers, workmen and more soldiers or guards were approaching, but they were under orders not to kill anybody unless they tried to cut the fuses.

Once all were over the brow of the big dune, Merriman turned, threw himself to the ground and covered his ears. Almost immediately the charges exploded and burning pieces of timber were flung high in the air. Merriman peeped over the ridge and saw that the hull of the part-built ship was burning fiercely, as was the frigate on the other side of the river.

The men ran back to the boats with no casualties, except for one man who stepped into a hole and broke his leg. He was dragged into a boat and, with lusty rowing from the excited seamen, they were soon back to the *Lord Stevenage* which was clearly seen in the light of the fires and the sparks flying up into the night sky.

Moving off shore, it was not long before they found Captain Anderson's ship and together they sailed to find the other ships out of sight of land.

When the senior officers gathered in the morning, Merriman related the results of the raid, paying particular attention to and congratulating Lieutenant Anderson on his part in the action. "Captain Egerton, sir, I hope your report to your superiors will lay emphasis on Lieutenant Anderson's actions. He played a vital role in our success."

"Again thanks to your planning, sir," replied Egerton to murmurs of agreement from the others.

"Maybe so," said Merriman, "but now we have to see what we can find in Beypore, our next target. After that, I think we should return to Bombay. So we must sail northward until we can find Beypore and see if we can do the same as we have just done." More approving murmurs met this, then he called, "Peters! Tea and coffee for our guests."

Peters and Tomkins had been expecting the order and very quickly the refreshment was forthcoming, after which the officers dispersed to their own vessels.

Chapter Twenty-Three

Mr Grahame starts enquiries

In Bombay, Grahame, in his professed task of investigating the state of the Company's army and the trading conditions under the threat posed by Tipu, was actively involved in talking to the senior army officers. Most were British, supported by Indian non-commissioned officers. He had sent a message ahead via the Governor's office to warn the commanding officer of his arrival and when his carriage drew up at the guardhouse he found a very smart guard company of lancers waiting with a British officer in command. The officer introduced himself as Captain Carter and said he had been ordered to meet Grahame and escort him to the headquarters.

Carter mounted his horse and rode alongside the carriage with some of the guard riding behind and some in front. At the headquarters, Grahame was introduced to the Commanding Officer, Major William McDowell. The Major apologised for General Stuart's absence, he had been called away to Madras to meet with the army's top command.

"Good morning, Mr Grahame, you are most welcome. It is not often that the regiment has a senior representative from the Government amongst them and I confess to being anxious to know why you are here. Sit down, sir. Might I offer you a glass of punch?"

Grahame declined but requested a cool fruit drink. The amenities settled, Grahame began his prepared story.

"I have been asked by Mr Pitt the Prime Minister to investigate certain matters here, not just about your army but also shipbuilding by that fellow Tipu Sahib who is making a nuisance of himself again. What I am charged to find out is how you feel about your army's readiness for war and how many men you have under arms. I know, Major, that you must send regular reports to Calcutta and they in turn send regular reports to

105

London, but it is felt that Calcutta only tells London what it thinks London wants to know. Sometimes those reports vary from information we receive from other sources."

"Well, sir, I can't tell you much about Tipu's shipbuilding but I do know that he is starting construction of a navy in several places down the coast. However, I can tell you what you want to know about the army. Currently we have about twenty thousand men and we are recruiting more every day. We hope to have at least twenty five or thirty thousand before Tipu gets up to his tricks again. They are mostly high caste Hindus and they have taken to their training very well, indeed they equal the best of the British Army. They are smart, excellent in the use of the musket, and have taken to drill and instruction marvellously. Of course most of them are foot soldiers but we do have a company of artillery, sir. The guns are dismountable for ease of transport on mules. And we also have some cavalry under Captain Carter."

"I must say, you are very enthusiastic about your men, Major, but have they been under fire?"

"Perhaps two thirds of them, sir. We were part of the armies which defeated Tipu in the last wars. All the native officers are as good as you will find anywhere."

"Very good, Major. I hear a lot of shouting outside, is it a drill or are we being attacked?"

He said this with a smile and the Major invited him outside to see what was going on. On the parade ground of stamped earth, three companies of Sepoys were executing their drill to the shouts of their native sergeants and under the watchful eye of the Subedar-Major, the senior native officer, who immediately and smartly saluted the Major. Another company of men was standing watching the drilling companies. From their appearance, they had only just been fitted out with their uniforms.

"That is the batch of latest recruits, Mr Grahame, but the ones out there are our best, trying to set an example to the newcomers."

The drill appeared to Grahame to be faultless. Every command was executed smartly and instantly, from simple marching, wheeling in formation and readiness for defence, lined up in three ranks, bayonets fixed and ready to shoot.

"Major, I must say that I have never seen better. They seem to be ready for anything."

"Indeed they are, sir. Would you care to inspect them?"

On the parade ground and under closer inspection the men were in perfect lines. Their uniforms were immaculate although covered in dust, but the Subedar Major accompanying Grahame and the Major growled a few disparaging remarks to a few of the men as non-commissioned officers have always done and probably would do in the future. The uniforms were a standard military coat worn over short trousers, cross belts across the chest supporting powder and shot, and a belt holding the bayonet and a small pouch. Each man wore a turban with a company or regimental badge on it. All men were barefoot and all were armed with a 'Tower' musket made in London.

"Major, I have spent some time in a guards regiment so I know what to look for and I haven't seen better until now. I think I shall have a glowing report for London."

"Thank you, sir, and now shall we go inside from this ferocious sun? I can see that the rain is nearly here as well."

As they made a dash indoors, the troops were dismissed and they too ran for their billets. The rain came down in torrents until one could hardly see beyond a few yards.

"When this has stopped, I'll take you over to the mess for a spot of lunch and to introduce you to some of my other officers."

"I would welcome that, Major, but first I have some more questions. Another reason I am here is to investigate spying among the Company staff and workers. It is suspected, in fact it is almost certain, that information is finding its way to these troublesome pirates. Captain Egerton of the Marine is sure of it. Have you any thoughts about it or have you seen anything out of the ordinary?"

"Can't say that I have, sir. Of course there are rumours and suspicions but nothing definite. We have a lot of native staff, cleaners, sweepers and the like, and they can go almost anywhere."

Grahame could learn nothing more and after lunch he left to go back to Bombay escorted by Captain Carter on his horse.

Chapter Twenty-Four

More enquiries & Grahame shot at

Grahame had rented a small bungalow with servants and a cook in the senior factors' residential area. After writing up his notes, he retired to bed, planning what he would do on the morrow though, before he got very far, he fell asleep. His sleep was fitful and the high humidity, the result of so much rain, meant that his sheet stuck to and tangled around him.

Next morning, after being shaved and wearing clean, dry clothes, a grumpy Grahame sat down to breakfast, still trying to decide what his next move should be. Finally, he decided to look around some of the factor's offices and warehouses. It should not be difficult; the factors knew why he was in Bombay and might be willing to talk to him and show him round their warehouses.

The Governor had lent him a small one horse carriage for his own use and, once his servant had made it ready, he set off. At each place he was warmly welcomed and shown around, several of the men even invited him round for dinner. On each occasion, after a good chat on the problems of business, Grahame asked the factor if any of his staff were often missing or behaving strangely, or if he knew if there were any Tipu's or pirate spies about. He made sure that he asked that question when junior factors and clerks were within earshot in the hope of stirring up something helpful.

After visiting several businesses, he returned to his bungalow to escape from the heat of the day and to consider what little he had learned. All except one seemed to be straightforward businesses, some dealing in spices, pepper, cloves, nutmeg and such. Others dealt in tea, rice, and opium and more with hardwood and various textiles, or indigo dye. In every case, the factors bemoaned the fact that they had too much stock stored because of fear of pirates. The only strange one was Mr

Goldberg. Of course it might have been because Goldberg associated him with Captain Merriman who had pointed out his ships' failings and cost him money, but even he was more affable when Grahame pointed out that he had been a mere passenger and nothing to do with the navy.

Grahame did notice that one of Goldberg's clerks sidled closer when spies were discussed, perhaps only by coincidence, but he did not believe in coincidences. That man would bear watching, he thought. Later in the day, after the regular rainfall, he visited more people using his little carriage but saw or heard nothing suspicious. He accepted one of the factor's invitations to dinner and spent a pleasant few hours with him and his family along with two other factors and their wives.

Arriving back at his bungalow, he handed the horse and carriage over to his servant and mounted the steps leading up to the veranda. Suddenly from the shadows a shot was fired, the ball passing close to his head and smashing into the doorpost. Immediately Grahame rushed inside. In the dark he scrambled for his own pistols then waited to see if anything else happened. Nothing did until his servants cautiously entered with lamps to see what had happened to the Sahib. He reassured them and told them to close the shutters before he went to bed with his pistols beside him.

His thoughts covered the events of the day from first to last, and the attempt on his life. Despite the attempt on his life, he felt rather pleased with himself. *Must have upset somebody somewhere today with my questions about spies,* he thought. *I wonder if that clerk of Goldberg's had anything to do with it. Perhaps I should tell the Governor and see if he can tell me where I can hire a bodyguard.*

He fell into a sound sleep, not wakening until his servant appeared with his morning coffee.

Chapter Twenty-Five

British Agents return to Bombay

Merryweather, his small crew, and Gupta made slow progress northward towards Bombay. The weather was not always kind to them; the rains repeatedly soaked them and the winds were not in their favour. Occasionally they saw other boats and made a show of putting their nets out, but the other boats kept well away from them.

"Just as well, Gupta, perhaps they thought we were pirates," said Merryweather.

Gupta had spent much of the time trying to teach him simple Hindi but Merryweather was finding great difficulty with it. To add to his irritations, he was sure he was developing a cold.

In the afternoon of the seventh day at sea, a ship was sighted. Hastily they put the nets out, pretending to fish and hoping the ship would ignore them. When it came closer they realised it was the sloop *Villain* which had dropped them off at the start of their adventure and they waved vigorously to attract attention.

"Welcome aboard, Mr Merryweather," said Lieutenant Johnson, captain of the ship. "We have been cruising up and down this part of the coast looking for you. You all look as though you need a good wash and a haircut. We can provide both but only a shower under the wash deck pump. Mr Williams, would you arrange that? Mr Merryweather can use my razor."

"Thank you, sir, these lice are the very devil. Perhaps I could have a shower now and these clothes, sorry, rags, be thrown overboard? I hope you still have my own clothes below. May I ask that you take our little dhow in tow? We might need it again."

Two hours later, Merryweather appeared on deck, washed, shaved and wearing his own clothes. His head was fully shaven to get rid of the lice and their eggs and he had started to feel more like his own self.

"I hope you are feeling better, sir. Your companions have all been washed down and shaved. Your own transport is being towed astern but if the weather gets too bad I'll have it brought aboard," said Johnson. "And now I'm sure you will need a meal and something decent to drink. I have a passable wine bought from one of the traders in Bombay to where we are making our way."

After the surprisingly good meal, during which neither of them spoke a great deal, Johnson asked if he could be told what had happened and what Merryweather had found out.

"A lot, Mr Johnson, a lot. We explored many small rivers and inlets but found nothing until we reached Bhatkal where we found some larger ships being constructed and at Mangalore, which is a hive of activity. Many ships being built there, mostly frigates I think but with some bigger ones, two decked, each one probably capable of carrying seventy guns or so."

"By Jove, our captains will be glad to hear that, sir. And now you may have my cot to sleep in, I have turned one of my lieutenants out of his berth so we can sleep comfortably. You look as though you need it."

Chapter Twenty-Six

Planning an attack on Beypore shipyard

Merriman's little squadron was making good time heading for Beypore, the weather had been kind to them and, apart from the heavy rains which were welcomed by the crew and which cooled everyone, nothing happened. Not even the odd trading dhow had been sighted or even a small fishing boat. Merriman had made a point of getting to know all the officers. Captain Egerton had invited him aboard for dinner on two occasions and as a result he now knew every one of them. He had taken Egerton's offer of a tour of his ship, the *Bombay,* and whilst not as smart as the *Lord Stevenage,* she was nevertheless a competent fighting ship.

When they reached the approximate latitude of Beypore, the ships hove to out of sight of land and Merriman left his ship in the capable hands of the First Lieutenant and boarded Anderson's sloop. As he had explained to Egerton, "I must have a good look at the place in daylight before we attack. The sloop will be seen but it should not seem to be unusual, just on a normal patrol."

Lieutenant Anderson was delighted to have Merriman aboard again and eagerly asked him what he had planned.

"We'll cruise along as close inshore as we can, from the south, slowly, so all your officers and as many others as you have telescopes for can study the place as we pass. I need to know everything that can be seen and then you can take me back to my ship."

The entrance to the Chulika river was very wide and obviously navigable well upstream as some large vessels, perhaps frigates, could be seen anchored on the starboard side. There was a busy shipyard and port on the opposite side. Anderson pointed out a fort built on a small headland overlooking the river. Not a very big fort but with the noses of what appeared to be heavy cannon poking out of the embrasures and commanding the river. Some men wearing red turbans were visible.

"A tempting target, Mr Anderson. I must give it some thought. Carry on northward and out of sight before we turn to find our other ships."

Merriman questioned the other men to hear if they had seen anything more. One thing that Merriman had missed was what appeared to be an encampment on the slopes behind the shipyard.

"Maybe some of Tipu's soldiers, sir. We know that he has overrun most of this coast and will want to defend the harbour," said Anderson. "Although there did not appear to be soldiers at Chettuva when we were there. But after we deal with this one, the whole coast that Tipu controls will be alive with soldiers, sir."

"I believe you to be right, Mr Anderson. I shall make plans accordingly."

Back aboard his ship, welcomed by all the usual ceremony, he sat in the great cabin thinking about the best way to attack. Peters came and went with coffee and then a meal, all of which passed unnoticed by Merriman, his mind was so busy. Unable to remain seated any longer, he went up on deck where everybody moved over to the lee side to give him room. He paced up and down, frowning and unconsciously tugging at his ear.

"I know that look," said Lieutenant Shrigley to the little Midshipman Green. "When he frowns and tugs on his ear like that he is devising some plan."

Suddenly Merriman paused, looked about him and up at the sails, but all was perfect. He found nothing wrong and nor did he expect to with the officers knowing he missed nothing. His thoughts were further interrupted by the big rain clouds and the beginning of the usual deluge. Back in his cabin, he decided he was hungry and shouted for Peters. When the man appeared, Merriman demanded to know why he had had nothing to eat since breakfast.

"But you did, sir, I brought coffee and food, sir, but you ignored it so I took it away, sir."

Seeing Merriman's angry face the poor man was in fear that he would receive some punishment, but Merriman's face cleared and he said, "I'm sorry, Peters, that was very unkind. It was my fault, and I was too deep in thought to notice. Now you must find the Master, the First Lieutenant and Captain St James, present my respects and ask them to be kind enough to join me. And you can tell the officer of the watch to signal for all captains to come as well."

When all were assembled and settled, Merriman began. "Gentlemen, I have devised a plan for action early tomorrow morning. Mr St James, the first part is for you and your marines to land at night and take the fort on the headland. Captain Little will take you ashore in his brig. I suggest that the two of you decide if the brig will have enough boats to do that, otherwise take one from this ship. When you have successfully secured the fort, fire off a red flare signal to seaward. If you can destroy the guns and the fort, do so, but if at all possible create as much damage as you can before retiring back to the ship. Any questions, gentlemen? No? Good."

St James just nodded his understanding of the orders.

"You, Mr Egerton, will wait with me out at sea until we see the flare, then the two frigates will enter the harbour with my ship leading. Now, you must remember that Beypore is a big trading port, the biggest and busiest on this part of the coast, and we must be certain that trading vessels are not harmed. There may be pirate ships mixed in with them, but, and I emphasise *but*, they will have to be left alone. Our objective is to create as much damage as we can on any big ships being built in the dockyard and on the three ships anchored on the other side which I believe to be frigates. Captain Egerton, when we are far enough inside, you go to larboard side and fire into the dockyard and concentrate on the big ships, then go about and repeat with another broadside, two if you have time. I will take my ship to pass the frigates and do the same to them. As long as the fort has been eliminated, we should be fairly safe unless there are any hidden guns. You, Captain Anderson, can lurk about outside and give us warning of any ships approaching. That is all, gentlemen, all you all sure about what must be done?"

Captain Egerton spoke, "An excellent plan, sir, but I believe there is a sand bar just beyond the narrowest part of the entrance and we should go in to either side of it."

"Thank you, Captain, we'll do that then," replied Merriman. "Before you leave, my servant will serve an excellent wine recommended by the Governor in Bombay."

Chapter Twenty-Seven

Marines attack the Fort

There was little but faint starlight when the boats grounded on the beach well out of sight of the fort. The marines waded ashore with muskets above their heads. Leaving a party of seamen to guard the boats, they began to climb up the dunes until they found the more solid ground of the headland. There, they took cover behind some low bushes and windswept trees to avoid being spotted. Mr St James and his sergeant crept forward, stopping at a point from where they could see the fort clearly.

"Idle buggers have left the gate open, sir, beggin' your pardon," whispered the sergeant.

St James inched forward a little more. "Can't see any sentries up there either, Sergeant. Go back and ask Lieutenant Goodwin to have the men load their muskets and fix bayonets ready, then fetch them up, quietly now. Tell them that if any man makes a sound he is in very deep trouble."

"Aye-aye, sir, they won't dare breathe when I've finished with them." He disappeared into the darkness.

Stealthy sounds could be heard as the marines loaded and then they moved forward.

"Pass the word, Sergeant, when we charge that gate I want no shooting unless absolutely necessary. Bayonets may be enough, and no shouting, no cheering, this must be done as silently as possible."

St James waited a few moments to allow the sergeant to repeat his orders and then he said to the men behind him, "Right here we go, come on."

The marines rose to their feet, diligently following their officer towards the gate and slipped inside the fort. A man, a guard probably, woke and started to shout a warning but his voice was quickly silenced by a marine with a well-judged thrust of his bayonet to the man's throat. The guard's shout and brief struggle had managed to wake another guard nearby who took a moment or two to decide what to do. By then it was too late, his hesitation cost him his life and he died by the ready bayonet of another marine.

"Lieutenant, I'll have some men on the ramparts and the others can spread out round the yard and check every doorway."

Again there was no sound from the garrison, and St James was beginning to think that success had been achieved with little bloodshed when shots erupted from a doorway. Two marines fell back dead as a large group of armed men burst out into the yard. Instantly fierce hand to hand fighting began, with the marines on the ramparts picking targets when they could. It was soon over, although the Indian soldiers would not surrender and to a man went down fighting. The brief fight had raised the alarm and St James noticed that more lights were appearing around the harbour.

"Sergeant, you know what to do, spike those guns and tip them over the side if you can. Mr Goodwin, you and your man with the fuse come with me now, we must find the magazine."

They looked into three or four doorways until they found one opening to a few steps leading down to a wooden door.

"This must be it, sir. There is a glass window in the door and a lantern hanging on that nail," said Goodwin. "I'll get the lamp lit and then we can see."

He carried the lamp up the steps and lit it. It was a very good brass lamp with glass on only one side and a tightly fitting door for safety. Goodwin held it up so that the light shone through the window to reveal a pile of kegs of gunpowder, one of which had been opened, the bung removed and the black grains of powder could be seen.

"Take the lantern as far back as you are able, Mr Goodwin, and I will open the door."

The door was fastened with only a wooden latch to avoid any sparking but powder could be seen scattered on the floor. St James sat down on a step, pulled his boots off and unbuckled his sword belt.

"Hold these for me, Lieutenant, and give me the coil of fuse."

Carefully he moved into the magazine. Without his boots there was no chance of a spark, but he took great care and gently pushed the end of the fuse into the opened bunghole, wedging it with an empty cloth powder bag from a nearby pile. Cautiously he retreated, uncoiling the fuse as he went until he was back in the yard well away from the magazine.

"Right, Lieutenant, give me the lantern and have the men assemble by the gate ready to go."

Pulling on his boots and his sword belt, St James realised that he could see more clearly. Dawn was breaking, revealing that the men were ready to go and carrying the bodies of the two dead marines. Opening the lantern, he applied the flame to the fuse and ran for the gate.

"Come on, men, as fast as you can back to the boats. Sergeant, have some marksmen ready to cover our retreat."

They scrambled over the dunes towards the beach and were nearly there when they heard a volley of marine's muskets firing. St James was relieved to observe that it was an organised and well-practiced retreat with regular files of marines firing and then scrambling behind the next file which fired in turn. They were nearly at the beach when with an ear-splitting boom, the fort exploded. Masonry flew through the air and St James saw the barrel of a cannon spinning end over end until it disappeared behind the headland. All of them reached the boats safely and the seamen were rowing strongly towards the brig when they saw the two frigates passing and moving into the river, a magnificent sight.

Chapter Twenty-Eight

The shipyard destroyed

The two ships had been waiting hove-to close off shore and Merriman, plus probably everyone else aboard, was anxiously watching for the signal flare. Just as dawn was beginning to lighten in the eastern sky, the fort exploded with a great roar.

"We couldn't have a better signal than that, Mr Cuthbert. Take the ship straight in."

"Aye- aye, sir," replied the portly Master, bawling out the necessary orders.

Everybody aboard was ready, the Topmen waiting to go aloft and handle the sails, the Waisters on deck to handle the sheets and braces, and on the gun deck every gun was loaded and ready.

Merriman watched keenly as the ship entered the river. "Mr Green, run below now, give my compliments to Mr Weston and Mr Shrigley, and that they can run the guns out now, but wait for the order to fire."

The boy scampered off and, looking down from the quarterdeck rail, Merriman was pleased to see all guns moving as one as the port lids were raised.

The *Bombay* kept close astern until, as planned, they separated to go either side of the sandbar. The wind was only a gentle breeze but enough to move the ships fast enough.

"Wind'll change in a few moments, sir," said Mr Cuthbert. "It should be enough to take us out again."

Merriman was watching and waiting for *the Lord Stevenage* to reach the anchored frigates which appeared to be anchored fore and aft, pointing seaward. Only one of them appeared to be ready for sea though. As he considered this, he was startled to hear the *Bombay's* guns open fire. She was already near the shipyards and, as he watched, Merriman could see baulks of timber shattering and splinters flying. A part-built ship collapsed as its supports were blasted away and another almost disintegrated. Egerton was controlling his broadside exactly, each gun finding a target.

Merriman turned as Lieutenant Andrews shouted, "One frigate is running out its guns, sir, but not a full broadside and the other two are not doing anything."

He saw this was so. "Probably only a skeleton crew aboard that one, David. We'll see."

As the *Lord Stevenage* closed on the manned frigate, Merriman shouted, "As your guns bear, fire."

The starboard guns erupted fire and smoke one at a time as they passed by, the balls smashing into the other ship, even as a second shot fired from the forward guns as they were rapidly reloaded. A few guns on the enemy frigate answered, some balls hitting the hull and others passing overhead. Then they were past it and ready for the next. That ship didn't even have masts rigged and the next broadside did immense damage to the stationary ship.

"Prepare to go about, Mr Cuthbert, as soon as we have passed the third one."

Again the starboard battery fired with no response and, as the ship turned, Merriman instantly reviewed the situation and had another idea.

"Mr Andrews, prepare a boarding party with some of our best seamen. I'll go alongside the first one and try to take it as a prize. Have a tow rope ready astern, we may have to tow it out."

"Aye-aye, sir," Andrews replied.

Once again the constant drill showed its worth. They had practiced for every conceivable event and, as they passed back and fired into the third ship, the boarding party was already assembling on deck. Another broadside hit the second frigate and then they were alongside the first. Ropes and grapnels were thrown and pulled in and the boarding party climbed aboard spoiling for a fight. The hardened fighting men were to be disappointed as there was nobody there left to fight; in fear for their lives they had all jumped overboard and were swimming to shore.

Andrews quickly saw what the situation was and yelled, "Topmen aloft, loose topsails and jibs. Three men on the wheel, and you and you find axes, be ready to cut the anchor ropes."

The crew of the *Lord Stevenage* had begun cutting the grappling ropes and, as the ship sheered away from the prize, Merriman shouted, "Is all well, Lieutenant?"

"Yes, sir, we'll be under way in an instant," Andrews replied.

"Well done, follow me out."

The *Bombay* had also turned and was almost abreast of the dockyard again when some hitherto hidden cannon opened fire. What damage was done, Merriman could not see, apart from a hole or two in the topsails. The *Bombay* continued to fire her starboard broadside, causing even more damage, and then she was past and following the *Lord Stevenage* and her prize.

Chapter Twenty-Nine

Turn back to Bombay

Later that day, all the ships stopped far from Beypore on the way north and the captains and their first lieutenants were rowed over to Merriman's ship. The usual ceremony due to the captains' arrival completed, they all gathered in Merriman's great cabin, chattering away until Merriman silenced them with an upraised hand.

"Be seated, gentlemen, I think a toast to our success is called for. Peters, you rogue, where are you?"

Peters and Tomkins were ready and a very palatable wine was served to all. Before Merriman could do so, Captain Egerton rose to his feet.

"Captain Merriman, sir, the adventure we have just completed has shown us all once again that your plans work perfectly, our objective has been completed, and you even took a prize. I never thought we would have managed to achieve all that we have. Captain Merriman, I must insist on proposing the first toast to you and your ship. Gentlemen, raise your glasses to Captain Merriman and his crew."

The toast was quickly drunk and Peters and Tomkins hastily refilled the glasses.

"Thank you, Captain and gentlemen, for that but you all played your part well. Captain St James and his marines destroyed the fort with the loss of only two men and five wounded, well done, sir." Applause died down and he continued, "Captain Oliver with his men did a first class task in landing the marines and collecting them again, and you, Captain Egerton, along with your men did all that we planned. Did you have any damage or loss when those guns fired at you? It was a surprise but I suppose not unexpected."

"No, sir, we were lucky. Only minor damage and only one man injured by a flying splinter. Did your ship have any damage?"

"Nothing of note," replied Merriman. "But sadly along with those two marines at the fort we lost a valued seaman from our boarding party. We buried them at sea two hours ago. Now then, the frigate we captured. I hope that the Company will buy it in for the Marine and all who took part in the action will receive prize money. And on that subject, I have an excellent prize crew aboard her but if you could spare a few men from your ships, it would be appreciated. I know that you, Captain Oliver, lost men in the defence of the convoy, so I won't expect any from you. So, gentlemen, I think we can be pleased with our efforts, and now I think we should now make our way to Bombay as fast as we can."

Chapter Thirty

Agents report to Graham

The sloop *Villain* slipped quietly into Bombay harbour. The midnight darkness was relieved only by the fitful light of a gibbous moon. No salutes were fired because, as Lieutenant Johnson told Merryweather, it was thought that gunfire in the night would awaken the town who would believe it to be an alarm. Merryweather was disappointed not to see the *Lord Stevenage* at anchor, but he decided to stay on board the sloop and visit the Governor in the morning.

Arriving at Government House, he asked for an audience with Governor Duncan. He did not have long to wait, the governor's secretary, Morgan, called him in to a warm welcome from the Governor who wanted to know what he had been doing.

"Only an exploratory cruise along the coast, sir, to see if we could find any more pirates, sir. We came back because supplies were running low."

"And did you find any?" asked the Governor.

"Nothing significant, sir," replied Merryweather, mindful of what Grahame had told him about spies.

"That's a pity, Lieutenant, what do you intend to do now?"

"Well, sir, I was hoping my ship would be here but it seems they are not back from escorting the convoy."

The Governor smiled. "No, it has taken longer than we expected but your friend Mr Grahame has rented a bungalow not far from here. I am sure he can find you a bed. Mr Morgan will show you where it is."

Merryweather approached the bungalow cautiously. The sight of three armed sepoys in front of it and two sturdy-looking men on the veranda armed to the teeth alarmed him. Was Grahame under arrest? When he got nearer he was relieved to see Grahame on the veranda, sitting in a lounger and talking to a small Indian man who quickly disappeared as soon as he saw Merryweather.

Grahame leapt to his feet and said, "I'm delighted to see you, Lieutenant. Come in, come in, to where it is cooler and have some refreshment."

When they settled, each with a cool glass of punch in their hands, Grahame asked Merryweather what he had discovered, commenting "I see you have lost your hair, sir. Lice was it?"

"Yes, sir, I had the devil's own job getting rid of them out of the stinking clothes Gupta provided for me. Well, sir, the sloop dropped us off ashore one night and we walked a long way until we reached a small town called Bhatkhal. There was some small local shipbuilding going on but nothing in the way of big shipbuilding. It was a different matter at Mangalore. There is a large shipyard there with three very big warships being built there, pierced for about seventy guns, and three others, frigates I think moored on the other side of the river. We were lucky to see so much before some soldiers appeared and chased us away."

Merryweather recounted how his disguise had worked. "I must have smelt like a cesspit, they all stayed upwind of us. We found a boat and we rowed down river, passing a big fort on the right hand bank. Then the ship picked us up again and brought us back here. Gupta was marvellous, I played the idiot and he passed me off as his imbecile uncle. He kept hold of the end of a rope around my waist."

Grahame roared with laughter. "I would have loved to see you, but you did well. Where is Gupta now?"

"Thank you, sir, I left Gupta back on the sloop. But what has happened here, sir, and why are you surrounded by armed men?"

"Somebody tried to kill me, that's why." Grahame recounted his actions over the last few weeks and that he must have upset somebody by talking loudly about spies. "The sepoys are from the Company army, the officer commanding insisted upon it. The two tough-looking men outside are my personal body guard. The Governor told me that they have sworn an oath to protect me with their lives and I could trust them."

"So it seems that you have made some progress in your enquiries, sir, and stirred something up. May I ask what you will do next?"

"You may, but I am at a bit of a loss. I need Gupta to help me and maybe you, in your disguise as a simpleton, can help too. Oh, I see that you have finished your punch, Mr Merryweather, would you like some more?"

"Yes please, sir, it is delicious, what is in it?"

"Well it is the favourite drink of most people here in India. It consists of tea, sugar, lemon, water and arrack which is quite a potent alcohol. Five ingredients which mixed together the people call Panch, Punch to the English. Mind you I don't have as much arrack in it as most people do."

"Well I must report back to Captain Merriman when he comes back but until the ship is here I cannot. I saw the Governor and he suggested that you might have room for me here, at least somewhere I could sleep."

"Of course, Lieutenant, there is plenty of room here. You are very welcome. The cook provided by the Governor is very good at his trade. There is an ample supply of food and the market is very near, so we won't starve."

Chapter Thirty-One

Merriman reports his success to the Governor

Once action at Beypore was over, Merriman found himself with time on his hands. Certainly he knew that the ship was in the safe hands of his Master and officers, the routine drills he had insisted upon were carried out regularly, and he resisted the urge to go on deck too many times in case the officers thought he didn't trust them. When he did go up, one sweeping glance told him that all was well. The result was that he spent much of his time alone in his cabin with his thoughts drifting back towards home.

Have I left my wife pregnant? If so I could be a father in a few weeks! A boy maybe to follow me into the navy, but it could be a girl. Well it doesn't really matter as long as Helen is well. I expect Mother has gone now and maybe Father as well. It could be months before fresh news reaches me out here.

Cursing himself for brooding and making himself miserable about things he could do nothing about, he went on deck where the heat struck him like a blow. Like all the officers, he wore only a shirt and breeches which were sodden in minutes. The ship was making a good speed with a fair wind but that wind didn't cool him down. The sky was absolutely cloudless although clouds would, as always, gather later in the day bringing heavy rain. Because of the rain, the crew was happy. They were able to wash their clothes which Merriman allowed them to dry on lines strung across the deck during the morning.

The ship was not far from Bombay at last, indeed Mr Cuthbert had predicted that only three days would see them there. A hail from the foremast lookout stirred everyone.

"Deck there, snakes, sir, lots of them."

The man shouted, pointing ahead of the ship. Merriman walked to the quarter deck lee rail and looked over. Every officer and crewman that could did the same. It was even so, a tangled mass of writhing yellow snakes could be seen, hundreds possibly thousands of them.

"Mr Cuthbert, you have been in these waters before, have you ever seen anything like this before?"

"Yes, sir, I have. They are called yellow-bellied sea snakes and at certain times of the year they congregate in large numbers like that. They are venomous but not aggressive and can be seen all over the seas off India and Oman and down to the Seychelle islands. I think it is something to do with mating, sir."

The ship was soon passed the slithering phenomenon and the chattering men went back to their duties.

Three days later, in the afternoon, the squadron entered the harbour at Bombay and the silence was broken by the thunder of cannon fire as salutes were made and acknowledged.

The prize crew on the captured frigate had roused out a spare anchor and all three frigates anchored in line, with the smaller vessels anchoring in their usual places near to where the sloop *Villain* had anchored. Merriman was pleased to see the *Villain* and he hoped that it meant that Merryweather had returned. Merriman's boat was in the water almost before the ship had anchored with its crew all smartly dressed, Williams the cox'n keeping his keen eye on them. Captain Egerton joined Merriman on the quayside and once again the Governor's carriage was waiting so the two captains were speedily taken into the Governor's office.

"Welcome back, gentlemen, welcome, and did you see any pirates? Was there a fight, were any convoy ships lost? I confess that we have been most anxious since you left. Damn it, I'm so excited I am forgetting the usual courtesies. Morgan, go and arrange for drinks at once."

Morgan disappeared, returning with a khitmatgar carrying drinks. Once they were settled, Merriman began.

"It has been a very successful round trip, sir. The weather was kind to us and we did have a fight with pirate ships but every ship in the convoy survived. We, that is the fighting ships, suffered very few casualties but the pirates were soundly beaten. They started with fourteen vessels of various sizes loaded with men. We sank all but one which escaped to tell the tale. We took no prisoners and hundreds of them drowned."

As he related all that they had done at Chettuva and Beypore the Governor became more and more excited, but Merriman noticed that Morgan's face fell as he heard of all the pirates' losses and the destruction of the warships being built for Tipu Sahib. He wondered why Morgan should be so downcast, but the man soon recovered himself and joined in the discussion.

"That is excellent news, Captain, and I see that you have returned with another frigate."

"Yes, indeed, we took it at Beypore and brought it home with a prize crew. I am hoping that the Company will buy it in for the Marine, Governor. The men from all the ships involved would welcome some prize money, I'm sure. It was damaged by our broadside but that will be easily put right, but it has not been fitted out with guns, partitions, stores and everything else needed. In fact it is only a shell and now it is here I need to take the prize crew back on board my ship."

"There should be no difficulty over that, Captain," said Mr Duncan. "We would welcome another ship, especially a frigate. Our dockyard should be able to deal with it. Now then, Captain Egerton, have you anything to add to Captain Merriman's account?"

"Nothing more about the details, sir, but I should like to recommend Captain Merriman most sincerely for his part. It was his advance planning and organisation which enabled us to achieve such success in everything we did."

"So noted, Captain Egerton, so noted. Captain Merriman, I will make sure that news of your deeds will reach the necessary ears at the Admiralty."

"Thank you, sir. May I ask if there is any news of Mr Grahame, Lieutenant Merryweather and the man Gupta?"

"Indeed yes, Captain. Mr Grahame has rented a bungalow and Merryweather is staying there with him. Morgan will show you the way."

Chapter Thirty-Two

Planned exposure of Pirate informers

Arriving at Grahame's bungalow and worried to see the armed men, Merriman and Egerton were welcomed warmly and put at ease by Grahame and Merryweather. Everybody told of their adventures, Merryweather again raising a laugh when he related the story of his disguise and the lice.

"Once again it seems that we have all done well. The pirates have been dealt a great blow which should keep them quiet for a while and, with several of Tipu's ships destroyed, it might be some time before he can get a fleet together," said Grahame. "But there are many things we still have to do. Captain Merriman, I suggest that we all meet again tomorrow morning aboard your ship, sir. I would not be too happy discussing our plans in the bungalow. One doesn't know whose ears may be listening."

And so it was arranged. All came aboard *Lord Stevenage*: Captain Egerton and his First Lieutenant Wilde, Merriman and Lieutenant Andrews, Grahame, Gupta and Merryweather along with the Marine Captain, St James.

Mr Grahame opened the discussion. "Gentlemen, as we all know our orders from London were to find out about Tipu's fleet building and to help the Company in their fight against the pirates. We have done all that but not all the possible ship building places our French pirate captive Dumont told us of have been investigated and I am sure that he knows more than he has told us. I would like to talk with him again. We know that there are spies here in Bombay. It was proven to be so, otherwise how on earth did those ships know when to attack the convoy? Other small convoys have been attacked and the pirates seem to know where to catch them. It would take too long to go from here to the south of the country by road, therefore the spies, or at least the information, must go by sea. As you have heard, I have been attacked, so I must have worried somebody. The prisoner is still here, James, is he not?"

"Yes, sir. He is confined below at night but I have allowed him some time on deck every day. I'll have him brought up at once. Captain St James, will you see to that please?"

A few minutes later St James appeared again, followed by a very apprehensive Dumont escorted by two burly marines. Merriman and the others looked the man up and down before Merriman said, "Thank you, Captain, I think your men could wait outside. Lieutenant Dumont cannot escape even if he wants to. Am I right, m'sieur?

"Oui, Captain, I will not escape, I don't want to. I know you could have me hanged as a pirate but I feel safer here than I did among the pirates. What do you want of me?"

"The truth! What you told Mr Grahame when we captured you has for the most part been proved correct, but I don't think you told us everything you know about the pirates hiding places, or the spies they must have in Bombay. Now then, what else do you know?"

Dumont took a deep breath, looked at all the men facing him and said, "While I was with the pirates I saw many different men from trading ships looking for Den Bosch, the leader of those cutthroats. I don't know what these men told him but I think they must have been his spies. Soon afterward he sent ships out loaded with men. Those ships came back with plenty of trade goods, obviously stolen. Den Bosch is a violent man and will kill anyone who opposes him, but because he is able to take so many ships, the men will do what he wants them to do. He is a devil. I saw him kill one man because he spilt some wine on his shoulder, stabbed him in the throat without getting to his feet."

"All that may be true and I don't doubt it, but do you know or can you recognise any of the men who come to see him?"

"I may be able to, but I saw them only briefly and may not recognise them. One of them is a white man and is the captain or owner of his trade ship, I don't know which."

"That is interesting, Dumont. Do you know if he comes from Bombay?" asked Grahame.

"I think so, sir," replied the Frenchman, "but I would recognise him if I saw him again. One other thing, sir, Den Bosch boasts that he has a frigate. I don't know much about it or where he keeps it. I think it may be one of two that brought volunteers from Isle de France to support Tipu's army. One of them left again but the other disappeared and may be the one Den Bosch boasts about. If it is, he must have persuaded the crew to join him or killed them all."

"Thank you, m'sieur, I think that will help us. Captain, have him taken out."

When the prisoner and escort had left, Grahame said, "We must act on this, but not too precipitately. We need to know more. I think we had better take our tame Frenchman ashore, in disguise of course, and see if he recognises the man. Do any of you gentlemen have anything to add?"

They all sat quietly for a few moments before Merriman said, "I have a suspicion, Mr Grahame, but only that and no proof. Captain Egerton, do you remember when we were with the Governor to report on our actions, did you notice anything strange about his secretary Morgan? No? Well I thought he seemed very upset and downcast when he heard about the pirate's losses but he quickly recovered himself and joined in the conversation. Why would he not be happy if a lot of pirates were killed?"

"A good point, Captain," said Grahame. "Maybe he is the man the Frenchman saw. I have another point. You know I was attacked and shot at, well that followed on my discussion with Mr Goldberg and my comments about spies. I noticed one of his clerks was too interested and moved closer to hear. He should be watched too. I don't suspect Goldberg himself, I don't think he is clever enough to be involved, but I think our course of action is now determined. If you are agreeable, Captain, and if Mr Merryweather is willing, he could disguise himself again and with our friend Gupta go into the town and the warehouse area to see if they can find out any more."

Chapter Thirty-Two

Informers caught

Gupta procured more native clothing for Merryweather and, later that night, they were taken ashore, quickly disappearing into the darkness. Merriman and Grahame sat up late that night discussing their plans. They finally resolved to take Dumont ashore and walk him round outside the governor's offices in the hope that he would see Morgan.

So, next day, Merriman went ashore with Lieutenant Andrews and Dumont, who was dressed in clothing from the ship's slop chest and provided with a wide brimmed hat as disguise. He was to pose as Merriman's servant and it was pressed on him that if he saw anybody he recognised he was not to reveal it.

Sure that they would be watched, they set of on a tour of the islands of Bombay with Dumont following meekly behind. Grahame's two bodyguards also attached themselves to the party. They wandered round the entire business district looking into several warehouses and ending up near the Governor's offices. There Dumont was trusted to wait outside, as a servant would, whilst they went in to see Mr Duncan who as always was pleased to see them.

"Welcome, gentlemen. Morgan, be so good as to call for refreshment for our guests. Have you any more plans afoot that I may know about and can I help? Not that you seem to need my help, you have all worked wonders at sea since you arrived, Captain."

"Nothing definite planned as yet, sir, although we shall take a cruise down the coast again. Who knows what we might find. There are many small rivers that we have not investigated and with luck we might find that devil Den Bosch. With all the losses we have inflicted upon him he must surely have to do something desperate to show that he is not beaten."

"Mr Grahame, are you any nearer finding out if we have spies for the pirates here?"

"No, sir, I am not, although I am certain there are some. I am at a loss to know what to do next. And now, Governor, we must leave you. You are a very busy man, sir, we shall intrude no longer."

"You are always welcome, gentlemen, especially if you can bring me some cheering news. Morgan, will you please show our visitors out and you could show them the new work going on to fill in some of the waterways to join some of our islands together."

Morgan escorted them out and walked them to the sea front where he showed them the constant stream of women with baskets on their heads carrying soil and rock for the development. Grahame's bodyguards followed behind with Dumont trailing behind them.

"Come on, man, don't dawdle. I want to get back on board. Hurry yourself and use the flag to signal for the boat," Merriman snarled at him.

"Aye-aye, sir, coming, sir," replied Dumont, acting the underling perfectly.

They were quickly back aboard the *Lord Stevenage* and in the great cabin.

"Now then, M'sieur Dumont, have you anything to tell us, did you recognise anyone?"

"Oui, Capitan, yes I have. That man who showed you round. I have seen him in a tavern talking with Den Bosch, down in a place called Chettuva where he keeps some of his ships."

"Did you, by God? We attacked Chettuva only a few weeks ago. He wasn't there but we destroyed some of his ships. Thank you, m'sieur, you have been very helpful so I don't think we shall hang you, at least not yet. Sentry, pass the word for the prisoner's escort."

"So you were right, James, Morgan is the one. He is in the best place to know when ships are sailing and you mentioned that he has his own ships and he travels south in them on occasion. He must have men that he can send to Den Bosch if he can't go himself. Well, we must wait for your Lieutenant to come back and tell us if he has found out anything that will help us round up Morgan's henchmen. Remember the old saying, James, 'An open enemy is better than a false friend.'"

The normal routine aboard continued with the crew engaged in the multitude of tasks needed to keep the ship in readiness for action. Merriman allowed shore parties of reliable men under petty officers to look around the markets. Merryweather and Gupta returned two days later, eager to tell where they had been and what they had seen. Merryweather was still dressed as a smelly beggar and he and Gupta showed everybody how they had passed as locals.

"Excellently done, Mr Merryweather. Get cleaned up and put your proper uniform on, then report to my cabin. Gupta, why don't you look as dirty or smell as bad as Mr Merryweather?"

"Easy, sahib, I have to look after him. He is lunatic and never washes. People smell him and keep away."

The lieutenant, washed and dressed, soon joined them, full of excitement as he told Merriman and Grahame what they had done.

"We found four suspicious characters, sir, one in Mr Goldberg's warehouse as you said. He met with three others from different warehouses all trying to look inconspicuous when they met at the arrack shop. We must have looked like part of the surroundings as they didn't seem to notice us."

"Very well done, Lieutenant, I will see to it that you will have special mention in my reports. And you as well, Gupta, you have done more than we hoped. Mr Grahame, what do you feel that we should do next? I think we should arrest Morgan and the other three men and after that I must sail south to see if I can find this fellow Den Bosch and his frigate and bring him to account."

"Yes, James, that we must do."

So it was that that evening Gupta pointed out the four men to a company of sepoys with Lieutenant Carter and a davidar or sergeant in command. They quickly arrested the men and took them away to the army camp with the sergeant keeping a close eye on them.

Merriman and Grahame watched all that activity, then, satisfied that all had been conducted properly, made their way to the Governor's office and requested to see him. Grahame's two tough body guards were with them and he instructed them to stay out of sight but near the office. A servant ushered them in to find Duncan and Morgan engaged in sorting out a pile of paperwork.

"Gentlemen, I'm surprised to see you again so soon, and armed I see. What is happening?"

Merriman answered, "We thought it best to be armed in the streets, sir, in case Mr Grahame was attacked again. We have found three men we suspect to be spies, clerks in some of the warehouses, but we still have to find out who it is that employs them. We have a good idea who it is but... Mr Morgan! Don't you want to hear more?"

Morgan was moving slowly towards the door and Merriman saw him pick up a sword leaning against a chair. He quickly drew his own sword, as did Morgan, and then there was no sound but for the clash of blades. It only took a moment, Morgan was not skilled with a sword and Merriman's blade quickly pierced his arm. Morgan dropped his sword and gripped his arm from which blood was seeping.

Governor Duncan was aghast. "Morgan? It can't be Morgan, he has been my secretary for years and I have trusted him. Captain Merriman, what do you know that I don't?"

"Plenty, sir, we have no doubt that he is the spy and that he reports ship movements to Den Bosch."

"It's a lie, sir, I've done no such thing," yelled Morgan as he dashed for the door, flung it open then stopped dead.

Grahame's two men were outside and they instantly seized him, pushed him to the floor and put the point of a sword to his throat.

"I think his own actions have betrayed him, Governor. An innocent man would not have used a sword or tried to escape. At least he would have wanted to hear what evidence we had."

Mr Duncan sat down with a thud. "I can't believe it, Captain. Will you please tell me what evidence you have?"

"I will do so, sir, but first I think Morgan should be removed," said Grahame, nodding to his men who picked the wretched Morgan up and marched him off, closing the door behind them.

Grahame and Merriman told Duncan the details of the investigation, that Morgan had been seen with Den Bosch and that Morgan's four men had denounced him, well, three of them did, the other was killed as he tried to escape. The Governor seemed to shrink as the details were related to him.

"My God, I can hardly believe it even now. How did he, why did he do it?"

"Money I expect, sir, that is the usual cause of treachery. Perhaps you could arrange for his house to be searched, sir."

"Most certainly, I'll go with you right away."

Outside they found Captain Carter with the rest of his sepoys and left Morgan in their capable hands, first emptying his pockets and taking his keys. The three of them walked to Morgan's house with Grahame's men close by. It was only a short walk and when they got there they found the doors wide open and not a single servant to be found. Nothing out of the ordinary was found until a large commode was moved to reveal a large steel safe. Morgan's keys soon had it open and the men stood back in amazement. There were boxes of gold and silver coins, gold ornaments and two large boxes filled with jewellery sparkling in the lantern light.

"Gentlemen that is all the proof I need. The man would never have collected such wealth from legitimate trade and the Company did not pay him this kind of money. Most of it must have come from his liaison with pirates, the gold and jewels especially. All this must be taken to my office as soon as possible; I have a bigger and stronger safe there. He will have a fair trial as the law demands, but I think he is doomed."

Chapter Thirty-Three

Ships sail again, ruthless search once more

Two weeks later, the *Lord Stevenage* and the five Company warships were again headed south to try and find Den Bosch and the rest of his followers. The bomb ketch had been left behind as it did not have the speed of the others. Gupta was with them and had told Merriman about more small harbours that they could search, although many of them would be too small to hide a frigate. Merriman had invited the officers from the Company ships to dinner and spirits were running high at the thought that they may find more pirate vessels including the mysterious frigate.

At the end of the meal, Merriman called for silence. "Gentlemen, I appreciate your excitement but may I remind you of an old dictum, 'he who would skin the bear has first to catch it'. This will not be easy. If we find them, they will fight to the end and we will have losses, maybe heavy ones. I propose that the two frigates stay offshore but in sight of the sloops which will go as close inshore as prudent to see what may be found. If we find that frigate, it may have most of the French crew still on board. They will be used to handling both the ship and its guns but I have no doubt we shall prevail. They haven't had the practice that my men have. If they have been hidden away, not going to sea for months, they will have lost their sharpness, and if half the crew is Indian and not used to handling a big ship, so much the better."

He paused and took another sip of wine as he looked round at the now serious faces.

"I should think it likely that, if we find it, there will be many other ships with it, small or large and they will also have to be dealt with. I will take the frigate and you, gentlemen, must try to take or sink as many as you can, but don't get too near. If they board you it will be savage fighting. If there are not too many of them to deal with, some of you could perhaps assist my ship. That is as far as I can plan. Are there any questions?"

It was a thoughtful group of officers that dispersed to their own ships, perhaps only just realising what they would be facing. Few of them had been in a major sea battle and it would be a baptism of fire for many of them. Merriman could only hope that they would rise to the occasion.

Chapter Thirty-Four

Violent gale, ships damaged

Their search was underway, but no quick results were forthcoming. That night, a violent gale arose and, in the maelstrom of shrieking wind, torrential rain and enormous waves battering the ships, there was no hope of keeping them together. Merriman had lookouts both aloft and on deck, replaced every hour with fresh men, but nothing was seen. The storm was so powerful that they could only run before it under bare poles and a single jib, the helmsmen lashed to the wheel and struggling to keep the ship straight. Merriman could not know how the other ships were faring and could only hope that they would come through safely.

The gale blew itself out as dawn broke and the near frozen and soaked lookout at the main topmast cross trees shouted down, "Deck there, I can see only one ship, sir, the frigate."

More sail was set and the *Lord Stevenage* slowly clawed her way down to the other ship's position. It was the *Bombay*, missing her fore top mast but with no more obvious damage to be seen. They were nearly together when the lookout shouted down again, "Sir, one of the brigs is out there." He pointed beyond the *Bombay* to where a ship with only one mast was rolling wildly. It could only be seen when it rose on a wave and then disappeared in the trough of the next wave.

When they reached it, Merriman could see that it was the brig *India Sun,* listing heavily with the wreckage of its top hamper dragging it over. A few figures could be seen desperately hacking away at the cordage holding the ruin of the mast to relieve the ship of its weight but it made a sorry sight.

"Mr Cuthbert, come up to that ship and give her our lee. We must find out how bad their damage is."

The Master bellowed the orders and the *Lord Stevenage* passed the stricken ship until they came between it and the still heavy wind creating a lee. An officer waved from the ruin of the ship and Merriman used a speaking trumpet to shout, "How badly are you damaged?"

The officer shouted back, "We lost the captain and a lot of men when then the mast came down. She is leaking like a sieve, sir, and I don't think she will last much longer."

"Mr Andrews, find some volunteers to take a boat down to that ship. I want to save as many as are left of the crew."

"Aye-aye, sir." Andrews turned away, bellowing for Matthews and a crew for the boat.

It was no easy task to swing a boat overboard due to the erratic movement of the ship but it was done and the boat was pulling hard for the for the damaged sloop when Andrews shouted, "She is lower in the water than she was a few minutes ago, I think she is going."

It was true and the boat barely managed to get clear with survivors before the ship turned over and disappeared rapidly below the waves. The miserable, wet and shocked crewmen, fifteen of them, were pulled from the waves and hastily given dry clothing. With a large tot of grog, they soon recovered. The only surviving officer was Lieutenant Graves, a mere slip of a youth, no more than seventeen or eighteen years old. Merriman took him down to the great cabin and gently asked him what had happened.

"The gale, sir, the worst I've ever seen, not that I've seen many. I was only appointed to the *India Sun* six months ago, sir."

He fell silent until Merriman said, "And then?"

The youth, startled, said, "I was on deck with Captain Little and Lieutenant Jones and other men, sir. The captain decided to get more sail off her and sent all our Topmen aloft to reef the main topsail. That's when it happened. The men were on the footropes and had only just started to furl the sail when the yard broke, then the mainmast snapped off and took the fore topsail with it. Not an instant later, half of the main yard swung round and fell through the companionway. It must have pierced the hull because we started to take on water. The captain was dead, sir, and so was the first lieutenant and many of the seasoned hands." He shook his head, looking down as he recalled the scene. "They had gone overboard with the mast and yard, the bos'n was knocked out and I was the only officer left. I put some of the men on the pumps but we were flooding too fast and the pumps couldn't cope with it. I confess, sir, it was all beyond me, I had no experience of that kind of thing and then we saw you, sir, and thought we had a chance. Some good men went down with her," he whispered.

"Do you think Captain Little held on too much sail for the conditions, Lieutenant?"

"I wondered about that, sir, but he was the captain, with far more experience than I had, so I cannot say if he was right or wrong. Maybe he did hold on too long or maybe the gear was rotten, I cannot say."

Merriman left him with a few encouraging words then went on deck to find the Master and First Lieutenant side by side looking back at the *Bombay*. "How are they doing, David? Can they clear the raffle and get her under way?"

"They are trying to get a spare spar aloft to serve as a new topmast, but all this pitching and rolling is making it very difficult, sir. They have stopped for now, waiting until the sea abates a bit more I expect."

The wind was easing and the great rollers were less fierce than they had been, but the ships were still lively. "Have we any damage, Mr Cuthbert?" asked Merriman.

"Nothing to speak of, sir, only a few ropes gone but already spliced. We have come through the gale better than I expected, sir…"

A call interrupted him. "Deck there, two more ships, sir, on the port quarter, I think they are ours."

Merriman had no cause to doubt him; the seaman up there must have sharp eyes to spot them. "Up you go, Mr Shrigley, take a glass and tell me what you see."

"Aye-aye, sir," Shrigley replied and climbed aloft like a frightened monkey. "The man's right, sir, two ships, a sloop and a brig. No damage that I can see from here. There is another one too, sir, further away, I think it is the other sloop."

By noon the next day, the small squadron was together, overall in reasonable condition. The crew of the *Bombay* were still finishing off the fitting of the new topmast but Captain Egerton had reported that his ship was again ready for action. The two sloops and the brig all had damage and reported the loss of some of their crew.

When the weather had moderated sufficiently, Merriman signalled for all captains to come to the *Lord Stevenage*. When all were seated, he said, "Gentlemen, I think we need to go back to Bombay for a refit. All of you have sustained some damage and in another gale may have more without a dockyard inspection."

There was a storm of protest, all of them insisting that their ships would be ready to meet whatever threat the weather could provide, but Merriman overruled them. "I know you are all disappointed, but there is another reason for me to go back. As you know there is to be a trial of Morgan and the rest. It is important that Mr Grahame and Gupta, together with myself and our Frenchman, are there to give evidence. The Governor said it would wait until our return but this is an opportunity to get it over as soon as possible. It is also possible that the other Company frigate may have arrived back from Madras. It would be a valuable addition to our little fleet."

Chapter Thirty-Five

Return to Bombay for trial and punishment

As Merriman had instructed, yet with some reluctance amongst the captains, they turned back towards Bombay. When they finally anchored in the bay at Bombay they were pleased to see the extra frigate *Madras* was there. Merriman and Grahame made their way to Government House where there was no delay in taking them to see the Governor.

The poor man had changed whilst they had been away. His hair had more grey in it, his shoulders bent and his face was more lined. He greeted them courteously but they were shocked to see the difference in him.

"I know, gentlemen, I know, I am not the man I was before you left. Without Morgan, much more work falls to me and there is always the worry about more spies and Tipu's intentions. Please tell me if you have some good news."

"Nothing new, sir, we were beset by a violent gale in which we lost the brig *India Sun* and most ships were damaged, so I judged it best to return here for proper repairs. Of course there is also the matter of the trial," said Merriman.

Grahame nodded in agreement.

The Governor sighed. "Yes, of course. Now that you are all here, I will arrange for the trial to take place in the early morning of the day after tomorrow and get it over before Christmas. The prisoners are still prisoners and the witnesses should be ready. Not a pleasant experience, gentlemen, but it must be done. I'll be glad when it's over."

The morning of the trial dawned and Merriman, Grahame, Dumont and Gupta were rowed ashore where a large carriage awaited to take them up to Government House. Inside, a large room had been fitted out to be as much like a courtroom as possible. The four of them were led through it, surprised to see plenty of people already sitting there. The men were invited into a small adjoining room where the Governor joined them.

"A sorry day, Captain, a sorry day. I would like to ask you to remove your best coats but I hope the punkahs I have arranged will help to keep the room cool. I shall not be the judge today. General Stuart has returned in time to take that office. He is after all the military commander of Bombay, which is more in keeping with regulations and of course means that I shall be a witness."

They sat in silence for an hour at least before an Indian in a black gown, a court official, asked for Mr Grahame to follow him into the courtroom. One after another they were called in, Merriman next then the Governor, then the Frenchman Dumont and even Gupta, to give evidence. Through it all Morgan sat in a chair, white-faced and trembling with two Sepoys guarding him. The three Indian prisoners were kept apart and likewise guarded. A jury of army officers and merchants had been summoned and all looked shaken by what they had heard. Finally General Stuart asked them to leave the room to consider their verdict. They were back very quickly with the only verdict they could give which was guilty.

"Thank you, gentlemen. Now, before I pass sentence, do any of the prisoners have anything else to say?"

The court official spoke to the three Indians in their own language but after a short dialogue they started shouting. The official spoke to them again after which they shook their heads and stared miserably at the floor. "Nothing, sir, they have nothing more to say in their own defence."

"Very well then, have the soldiers bring the three of them to the front for me to pass sentence."

The men were lined up in front of the general.

"I know that you all understand what is happening here and you also know what could happen to you. You have all betrayed your Factors and the Company and passed information to the pirates but I know you were seduced by this other man and his promises. You will not be hanged but you are sentenced to work in the Company's quarries, in chains, for the next six years. Take them away."

Merriman and the other witnesses waited in silence while the prisoners were dragged away and until the excited chatter of the spectators had died down. The General banged on his desk and called for immediate silence, banging repeatedly with the gavel until an expectant silence hung over the room.

"The prisoner will stand. Mr Morgan, you have heard all the evidence against you, have you anything to say before I pass sentence?"

The trembling man shook his head not saying a word.

"Very well then, you realise that there is only one sentence you can expect for your crimes and that is death. So I sentence you to death, not by hanging but by firing squad immediately at the rear of this building." The general frowned at the audience. "And there will be no spectators. Captain Carter, take him away and see that the sentence is carried out without delay."

Knowing the likely outcome of the trial, all must have been arranged beforehand because after only a short wait the crash of musketry was heard. It was all over. The subdued public dispersed and the Governor told Grahame and Merriman that the General wished to speak with them.

When they had gathered in the room adjoining the courtroom, General Stuart said, "I wish to thank you both for all you have done in this whole sad affair. From what I have been told, if Morgan had not been caught, more information would have found its way to our enemies. Congratulations and thank you. I would like to ask you to dinner in my quarters but I understand that the Governor has arranged a dinner for Christmas Day and you will be sailing again in a few days afterwards if all repairs are completed, is that right?"

Merriman nodded. "Yes, sir, it is. We want to try a different plan to catch the mysterious Den Bosch who controls the damned pirates."

"Well good luck to you, my boy, and good hunting. I'll see you when you return to Bombay."

Chapter Thirty-Six

Christmas festivities

The Governor had indeed arranged for a lavish Christmas dinner at his residence to which all officers from the ships and the army had been invited, leaving the crew and only the necessary officers aboard. The crew of the *Lord Stevenage* had not been forgotten. A bullock had been roasted over a huge fire on the beach and the cooked meat was eagerly awaited on board. The governor had also supplied two barrels of wine to complete their pleasure. At the feast ashore, good wishes abounded with all the officers repeatedly toasted to their success. Many people fell asleep although Merriman kept a sharp eye on his own men to ensure that they did not overindulge.

For himself, the festivities, the food and drink, reminded him forcefully of Christmas celebrations at home. There would be a huge meal prepared by Annie, his mother's housekeeper and friend, the gifts and jollifications lasting well into the evening. But he was saddened by the thought that his mother may be dead, maybe his father as well. He pondered about what his new wife Helen would be doing, had she been pregnant when he left and was he now a father?

His gloomy introspection was interrupted by the Governor's wife who nudged him forcefully in the ribs. "Come, Captain, why look so lugubrious at this happy time?"

"Thinking of my last Christmas at home, ma'am, which was the last time I saw my parents. I know Mother may be gone now and I don't think Father would have lived long afterwards. I was also wondering what Helen my wife would be doing. Her father also is not a young man and he may be gone as well."

"Gloomy thoughts indeed, James," she said. "I may call you James, may I not? All you young men who serve your country abroad have left parents and family behind but what cannot be changed must be endured."

She signalled to a waiter standing behind her who swiftly disappeared to return moments later with a bottle wrapped in a cloth.

"This is one of my own choices, James. I hope it will cheer you up," she said as the servant deftly filled new glasses. "And here's to you, James, and your bride. Have you any children?"

"Not as yet, ma'am. We were married only a few weeks before I left but…" He smiled as he confided in her, "We were trying hard, so I don't know."

The evening passed in a whirl, there was dancing, more food and wine and conversation, so that the officers left the party in a gleeful state and made their way back to the ship.

Chapter Thirty-Seven

To Ceylon, Pirate base discovered

Two weeks later, the Company's ships, now reinforced by the extra frigate but still under Merriman's command, set sail for the south. Before sailing, Merriman called all the Company officers to his cabin for a final council of war. After Peters and Tomkins had provided refreshments Merriman began his prepared talk.

"You know, gentlemen, that the convoy was attacked soon after we passed the Maldives. We also know that several fishing boats saw us and quickly made off in the direction of the islands, from which I infer that the pirates were staying there. They could not have reached us so quickly otherwise. Do you agree with my thinking, gentlemen?"

"Indeed yes, sir," replied Captain Fitton of the *Madras*. "And another point, sir, is that if this pirate fellow really has got a frigate and other large dhows, they could not lie hidden there for long. They are only low lying coral islands with no hills."

"Quite so, Captain, therefore this is what I propose we do. We will leave your brig *Hannah* behind with the bomb ketch and Captain Oliver. There are still other pirates about and we must not leave Bombay without any naval defences. During the fight for the convoy you were boarded, Captain, and we now know that the pirates' main form of attack is to board and overwhelm crews with force of numbers. Do you all have boarding netting?"

All signified assent except for Captain Johnson of the *Villain* who said, "None aboard at present, Captain, but I'll scour the dockyard for something."

"Very good, and if you all have plentiful supply of boarding pikes aboard keep them well sharpened, there is nothing better for killing and discouraging attackers tangled up in the netting."

A murmur of assent went around the room.

"Finally, gentlemen, I propose that we sail in line abreast, with the sloops scouting ahead. We must all sail within signalling distance so if the sloops find anything of pirates or Tipu's shipbuilding, we can all close in. This expedition could take many weeks or even months because if we turn up nothing along the south coast of India I propose to sail across to Ceylon. So make sure that you have all the supplies you will need. Fresh water can be taken aboard at any suitable place. So there you have it, have any of you anything to add?"

Nobody did and, after another toast to the success of their venture, they all left, chattering about the dangers to come.

Nothing of pirates or big ship building was seen until they reached Chettuva where it seemed that some desultory efforts had been made to repair the ships damaged during their last visit there. A few dhows flying red flags were seen and quickly destroyed. The squadron moved on to the south round the curve of India until the land was all to the north of them. There they found a secluded bay where they were able to replenish their water casks and, whilst at anchor, Merriman took the opportunity to call all the captains together for another conference.

"What are your charts like of the coast on this side of Ceylon?" he asked.

Most of them could only produce sketchy charts showing little detail.

"Do any of you know anything about the place or any bays where the pirates can safely anchor?"

"I may do, sir," replied Captain Fitton of the *Madras*. "I sailed down here in a trading ship before I joined the Marine. There is a large bay protected by long sandbars and small rocky islands. I was only a boy then but I remember that there were several entrances to it, or exits too. I think the captain called it Portuguese bay and it must be about this latitude or near to. That is all I know of it, sir."

"Then I think we should investigate it further, gentlemen, if we have nothing else to go on," decided Merriman.

And so they sailed for Ceylon until one day a sharp-eyed lookout shouted down, "Deck there, land dead ahead, sir."

"Up you go, Mr Hungerford, and tell me what you see," Merriman ordered.

The youth settled himself into the crosstrees and scanned the coast ahead. "It seems to be a long, low land with thick jungle behind white sand beaches, sir."

"Can you see any sign of rivers or bays?" demanded Merriman.

"No, sir," the boy replied. "But I can see what I think is smoke further down the coast to starboard."

As the ships approached the land, Hungerford suddenly shouted, "Shoal water ahead, sir, we must turn to starboard."

Merriman waved to indicate that he had heard and turned to the Master saying, "Take us out, Mr Cuthbert, as fast as you can and put a good man in the chains with a lead-line. Mr Green, signal the other ships to keep off, shoal water ahead."

"My charts don't say much about here, sir," reported the Master, "but we should proceed with caution."

"Very well, Mr Cuthbert, we'll proceed parallel to the coast down to where Mr Hungerford thought he could see smoke."

Cautiously they proceeded until smoke could definitely be discerned above the trees.

"That will do, make to, all ships 'prepare to anchor', Mr Green."

The anchor splashed down and the sails disappeared like magic. As the *Madras* anchored, her gig was seen rowing hard for the *Lord Stevenage* with Captain Fitton in the stern.

"Side party, Mr Andrews, if you please," called Merriman and the usual honours were given as Fitton climbed aboard.

"What is the reason for your haste, sir?" asked Merriman as the other captain settled his sword correctly.

"I remember this place, sir. If you look a little to the right of the smoke you can see two of the pointed temple buildings they call a Dhagoba, sir, and near there is a good-sized village. If you look carefully you can see fishing boats drawn up beneath the palm trees and if I am right the bay we are looking for should be only a few miles north of here."

"That is excellent news, Captain. Come below and tell me more. Are the people here friendly and do they welcome strangers?"

"I believe so," replied Captain Fitton, "but as I told you it is many years since I was here. A lot could happen in that time. I should like to go ashore with some trade goods and your Mr Gupta. He may have some knowledge of the language."

Merriman stared out of the cabin windows as he thought about it. "Very well, Captain, you may go, but take good sized armed party with you. Any sign of trouble and you should get out as fast as you can. Of course what we need to know is: have they seen any big ships and where is this Portuguese bay you spoke of?"

Fitton rapidly returned to his ship and very soon a larger boat, filled with marines and armed seamen, was pulling for the shore. As the boat grounded, Fitton and some of the marines climbed out and onto the sand. As they did so a group of men appeared through the trees, one of them wearing some form of glittering headwear, and stood waiting for Fitton's approach. There was no sign of hostility even though Merriman could see that some of the men carried swords. Leaving a party of seamen and marines with the boat, they all walked into the darkness beneath the trees. Perhaps an hour passed before they returned to the beach and were brought off by the boat which headed straight for the *Lord Stevenage*.

"All went well, sir," reported Fitton. "They were suspicious at first but the gift of the trade goods soon calmed them down. I think it was the sight of your union flag that made the difference. They treated us well, offered coconut milk to drink and pieces of stringy chicken to eat, after which we started talking. Mr Gupta could understand a lot of what they said and we were told that a large ship had anchored in a bay up the coast, with many smaller ones."

Gupta revealed more of what had been said. "Bad mens over there, sahib, very bad. Raid village for food and took women. They say that boats carry red flags on their masts."

"Well done Captain, Gupta. We may well have found Den Bosch and his men, but we cannot do anything until we know more details about the bay and its entrances. It could be very risky taking our ships in there without soundings."

"I agree, sir, but the villagers said they would take us there and show us. They fish round there all the time and know the waters well."

"That is welcome news indeed. If we could go with them and make a brief survey and a few soundings of the best ways in and out of the bay, then we can make a plan."

Chapter Thirty-Eight

Planning an attack

The Dutchman, Den Bosch, was still uneasy. He had taken his frigate and his reduced fleet to Ceylon to anchor in a large, secluded bay which offered several ways in and out. Nothing had been seen of any other ships, frigates or otherwise, and he believed he had managed to find a safe place to stay. He had anchored in this bay many times in the past, knowing that his best defence was the shoal waters and reefs forming the seaward boundary of the bay where there were only three difficult entrances.

Nevertheless he was worried. If that British Navy frigate was after him he knew it would not give up the chase so easily and could eventually find the anchorage. Most of his Indian crewmen were sleeping ashore or not sleeping as the case may be. They had captured several native women from down the coast and were taking turns with them. Most of the original crew of the frigate had been French and many of them had gone with the volunteers to join Tipu's army. Only just enough of them had stayed to form the backbone of his crew.

Moreover, he knew that if it came to a ship-to-ship battle with a British frigate, he was bound to lose. Not enough time had been given to training the crew in gunnery and ship handling, which was his own fault. Although he was certain that his men would fight desperately, knowing their fate if captured, he knew that his ship, the ex-French frigate *La Marveilleuse*, was no match for a better handled ship. What should he do?

A thought struck him. If it came to the worst he might, with a few good men, find his way ashore and escape. The natives would not bother them. He therefore resolved to gather together the most easily carried part of his share of the booty, jewellery mostly, and if the British ship showed up, to confide his plan to the few men he thought he could trust. Even that was taking a risk. He strode about his cabin in an agony of indecision, what would be the best thing to do?

Meanwhile, two of the more easily paddled canoes from the village, the first with Merryweather and another seaman aboard alongside the native crew, the second with two well-bronzed sailors amongst the fishermen, left the village and headed for Portuguese Bay. They arrived at the south entrance as dawn was breaking. There they made a great show of throwing out their nets for fish whilst the sailors surreptitiously dropped their lead-lines overboard and recorded the results. They were far enough away from the pirate vessels for their actions to be clearly seen and made rapid progress with the soundings.

The *Lord Stevenage* and the Marine ships had moved safely out of sight, with Merriman trying hard not to show his concerns to the crew.

About mid-morning, the two canoes, with a load of fish aboard, moved up to the north entrance of the bay and slowly continued with sounding the depth of the water. At last Merryweather pronounced himself satisfied and the canoes made their way back to the village.

When the ship's boat brought him back to the *Lord Stevenage,* Merryweather was keen to show the results of the survey to Merriman. The figures showed ample depth of water even at the estimated low tide, for the frigates at the north and south entrances. The centre entrance though showed very shallow water with only a narrow channel weaving its way between lumps of coral.

"Very well done, Lieutenant, very well done." Merriman smiled then asked, "The pirate vessels showed no interest in you, is that correct?"

"Yes, sir, I could only see the tips of the biggest ships' masts, so I don't think they knew we were there."

Merriman spent the next few hours planning, and going over the plan time and time again to ensure that he had forgotten nothing, tugging at his ear all the time. Then he called for Merryweather and Gupta.

When they arrived, he asked, "Do you think the natives will fight the pirates?"

"Yes, sahib, they will. They don't have muskets, only spears and bows, but they will fight if you can help them," replied Gupta.

"Good. I want the two of you to go ashore again and tell them what I propose to do, which is…"

He outlined his plan and the two men left whereupon Merriman signalled for all captains to come aboard. The four of them arrived in a fever of anticipation to know what Merriman had learned and planned.

"Gentlemen, I believe I have a sound and workable strategy to engage the enemy forces and, if you each play your part as I will lay out for you, then I think we can finish the matter in the morning. Gather round and look at my sketches, this is what I want you to do."

Chapter Thirty-Nine

Final battle, Merriman is wounded

Long before dawn, the two sloops took on the marines from the two Company frigates. Then, creeping slowly through the north and south entrances to the bay, or gates as Merriman was now calling them, the marines were quietly deposited on the shore, well away from the pirate fleet. There they were greeted by the local natives armed with bows and arrows, spears and knives, led by Merryweather in the north and Gupta to the south. They crept forward until they were surrounding the enemy camp. Then they waited. One or two sleepy pirates roused go in the bushes to relieve themselves but were made to "disappear" without trace or any warning noises given.

One after another, the two Company frigates crept through the northern gate, making hardly a sound as they drifted down towards *La Marveilleuse* and the attendant dhows, desperately trying to maintain the element of surprise. Suddenly, somebody, a guard maybe, roused himself to shriek a warning to his fellows. But it was too late. Both frigates rounded to and opened their gun-ports and, as one, the ready-loaded cannon released a hail of death and destruction on the anchored pirate frigate.

Screaming men, taken by surprise and woken from their drunken haze, ran here and there, not knowing what they were doing. But some men, probably the French, were more organised and quickly sent men aloft to loose some sails and others for'ard and aft to cut the anchor ropes.

Another broadside crashed home from the two Company ships before the enemy frigate managed to move in the direction of the southern gate, seeking escape. The small dhows scattered, some trying to reach the middle gate but bleary-eyed and confused by the noise and the half-light, their crews ran them aground on the sandbanks and coral.

The two frigates passed by and loosed broadside after broadside as fast as they could into the helpless craft and screaming crews, then followed the pirate ship down to the southern gate.

On shore, as the groggy pirates were woken by the noise, they found their comrades transfixed by arrows coming out of the seemingly impenetrable jungle. Some tried to organise a fight, shouting, "This way, this way, we can escape here," or similar cries of encouragement. They were quickly dealt with and fell with several arrows sticking out of them.

Then the marines charged; their uniforms and flashing bayonets striking fear into the enemy. Merryweather and Gupta kept out of the way, not wanting to be confused as enemy by the enraged natives who slaughtered the pirates and began to hack and mutilate the corpses. Merryweather called to the marine officers, suggesting that it would be a good idea to press on southwards to see where their ships were. After some resistance by some of the marines who wanted to carry on looting the bodies, they began their march, leaving the natives to their gruesome work.

Aboard the *Lord Stevenage,* they heard the sounds of battle coming closer and soon saw the shape of the French frigate emerging from the smoke. *Lord Stevenage* was just where Merriman wanted her to be, like a cork in a bottle preventing the French frigate finding an easy way out to the sea. One of the Company frigates was following but held back on seeing Merriman's ship and knowing what would happen next.

Merriman's first broadside smashed into the pirate frigate, lethal splinters flew everywhere and the foremast simply crumbled. But some determined souls with fight left in them managed to get some guns working and, as Merriman ordered his ship alongside, they fired. A blast of iron and lead crossed *Lord Stevenage's* decks and men shrieked in agony as they were cut down. Merriman dragged his sword out and ran forward shouting for boarders to follow him but there were still too many pirates opposing them.

"Fall back, fall back, men," cried out Merriman, almost sobbing as he saw his men cut down like so much wheat.

Now the boot was on the other foot and Merriman and his men were forced back and back until, with a huge explosion, the forward carronade fired, sweeping the decks clear of enemy resistance.

"Forward, men," bellowed Merriman.

His men poured after him as they felt a big thump and a shudder go through the pirate ship as the frigate *Madras* ground alongside the enemy ship.

It was soon over. Merriman cut down a maddened man who ran at him with a sword raised above his head with no attempt at defence. Merriman stared round him in a daze. Screams came from all sides as the remaining pirates were cut down. He saw Biggins, whose hatred of the French was legendary, pull his cutlass from the belly of a French pirate and shout, "Got you, you bugger, got you." He looked round for another victim but there were none. He saw Merriman and grinned. "We got 'em this time, sir, didn't we?"

Merriman felt the strain easing away then suddenly Captain Fitton was there in front of him.

"Congratulations, sir, congratulations, your plan has worked perfectly. These devils will attack ships and murder the crews no more. We have won a famous battle."

"I think we have, but at what cost? I have lost many good men today, ones I could not spare so far from home." He swayed and then found his cox'n Matthews supporting him on one side and Biggins on the other. "Dammit, I can manage, let me go."

They did so upon which he promptly collapsed on the deck, a fierce pain striking his leg. He looked down to see his left trouser leg sodden with blood. "I didn't feel that," he said and promptly passed out as a wave of searing pain struck again.

The next thing he knew was waking up in the orlop with Doctor McBride leaning over him and Lieutenant Andrews anxiously leaning over the other side.

He stared up at them, terrified that they were going to cut off his leg but then the doctor said, "Rest easy, sir, your leg is safe. It was a good, clean cut washed with its own blood. I've bandaged you and will have you back in your quarters as soon as I find somebody to carry you."

Immediately there was a storm of voices. "I'll carry him, sir," shouted a burly bos'n's mate. "No, you won't," shouted Biggins. "I carried 'im down and I'll carry 'im back up."

"If you are two determined on this, you must do it together and keep his leg away from hitting anything," the doctor told them.

Merriman was aware that the two men were carrying him, Biggins showing surprising strength for such a small man, until he found himself in his part rebuilt cabin where they gently put him into his cot. He saw the stricken faces of Peters and Tompkins then the world spun and he knew no more and was lost in darkness.

Finally he woke to see the sun shining through the windows and the ship moving gently, with only the creak and groan of its timbers to show that she was moving. He dozed again and then woke with the memories of the battle flooding his mind. He cried out and then Peters was there and the doctor was unwrapping the wound on his leg. The last bit of bandage came away with a gentle tug which made Merriman gasp. He saw the doctor sniffing at the bandage then he grinned. "All is well, sir, no indication of infection."

"Never mind me," snarled Merriman. "Tell me how the ship is and who have we lost."

"Rest easy, Captain, you have been flat on your back for the last three days. You lost a lot of blood and the body takes time to recover. The ship is under the command of your First Lieutenant and repairs are almost complete. He wants to see you, sir, but I kept him away until I was sure about your health. My little office has been besieged by men asking after your health. They think very highly of you, sir."

McBride finished wrapping a new bandage on Merriman's thigh and then said, "Shall I send him in now, sir?"

Merriman nodded weakly and said, "Yes, I must know…"

A moment later, a gentle tap of the marine sentry's musket on the deck sounded and his voice said quietly, "First Lieutenant, sir."

Andrews popped his head round the edge of the door, grinning all over his face at the sight of his captain awake. "The word has spread, sir, that you are awake. All the officers and others asked me to give you their best wishes for a speedy recovery."

"Yes, yes, man, but tell me about the ship. Is she repaired and how many did we lose?"

Andrews' face fell and he hesitated. "Ship's well, sir, only superficial damage and Mr Green the carpenter had all the hands working like madmen to do the repairs. He's been a tower of strength, sir. All ships are anchored in Portuguese Bay including the prize."

Merriman shifted restlessly, wincing at the pain. "Damn it, David, tell me about the men, how bad is it?"

Andrews' face fell even more. "Well, sir, we lost twelve dead and some fifteen wounded although the Doctor says that most of them will recover." He hesitated.

"Oh get on with it, man, you're shillyshallying like a woman on her wedding day," snarled Merriman.

"Yes, sir," Andrews gulped. "The dead include Mr Cuthbert, sir, and Mr Weston and Mr Hungerford. The rest are sailors and marines including the marine sergeant and Larkin, the man with the phenomenal eyesight. And two of Mr Egerton's officers were lost and several others of his crew, sir. We buried the dead at sea, sir, two days ago."

Merriman closed his eyes and groaned. "Not Mr Cuthbert, surely? Did you see it, David, did he suffer?"

"Very little, sir, a ball took off both his legs at the knee and he bled out very quickly. McBride told me that the shock of the injury would have stopped him feeling much pain. Captain St James saw him and was with him at the end and I believe he has a message for you. Mr Weston was shot down when he followed you aboard *La Marveilleuse* and young Mr Hungerford fell at his place by the signal locker. I'm very sorry, sir. Mr Cuthbert was very well liked by all and he was almost a father figure to us."

Merriman grimaced at the memory of how he had denied Cuthbert's request to bring his wife and daughters aboard to see where he lived, thoughtlessly denied because the ship was a hive of activity taking on stores, new men and equipment. Now he regretted it. He would have to visit them when he got back to England. It would be a terrible task.

He moved restlessly again and Andrews who had thought him asleep and was about to leave, leaned over and asked if he should fetch the Doctor.

"No, David, thank you. Leave me to think about it all but you could send Peters in with a drink, and ask Captain St James to see me."

St James duly presented himself with a huge smile on his face and a large bandage on his arm. "Can't express how delighted we are to see you recovering, sir."

"Yes, thank you. I am told that you were with Mr Cuthbert when he died, is that so?"

"Yes, sir, when I got to him he was nearly gone, he was losing so much blood you see, but his last thoughts were for the ship. He managed to gasp, 'Tell the Captain I'm sorry to leave him, but Master's Mate Henderson is well able to take my place.' Then he called out a name, perhaps his wife, sir. That was all, sir, then he was gone."

"I, we, shall miss him. He seemed to be a part of the ship." Merriman seemed lost in thought and St James thought he had gone back to sleep but Merriman stirred and said, "My compliments to Mr Andrews and will he come down and bring Henderson with him?"

When the two men appeared, Merriman got straight to the point. "Mr Henderson, you have had the strongest recommendation from Mr Cuthbert that you should take his place, you are well able to do so and so I am rating you as Master from this moment. You may still have to take another test before you are officially accepted by the establishment, but we'll worry about that in due course."

"Yes, sir. Thank you, sir. Mr Cuthbert taught me everything he could and I'll miss him too. I'll not let you down, sir."

"Didn't think you would, Master. Mr Cuthbert was always very sure of you. You can use his cabin and charts and all that but please put anything personal into a box and bring it here. Now go, and leave me with Mr Andrews."

When the very pleased man had gone, Merriman questioned Andrews about the Frenchman Dumont. "What are your thoughts about him, David? He has been of very great use to us and I don't want to hang him."

"No, sir, and none of the others want you to either. I have allowed him to join us in the wardroom a few times and he has made himself most agreeable. Also I took the chance of not having him shackled at any time, I'm sure he doesn't want to escape."

"My thoughts are the same, David. I'll have to decide what to do with him. If he wants to join us I've a mind to let him, or put him ashore somewhere in France if he wants that."

Two days later, Merriman had himself carried up on deck and installed in a chair under a sun awning. Looking keenly about him he could see no sign of repairs apart from some pieces of lighter-coloured wood used as patches. The four Company ships were close by, some repairs evident and *La Marveilleuse* still under repair. That reminded him and he called for Mr Andrews. "David, what happened to the crew of that ship and did you catch the captain?"

"We do have seven of them in chains below, sir. The rest were killed and all those ashore were killed by the natives. The only one missing is Den Bosch. I am told that he and four men rowed away to the top end of the bay before the attack started. He must have known we were coming, sir, and probably took his share of his loot with him. We found a ton of gold and silver and silks and cottons in the hold too, sir."

"Very good, we can take all that back to Bombay. The governor will know what to do with it. Is any effort being made to catch Den Bosch?"

"Yes, sir. The country there is thick jungle full of poisonous snakes and I don't know what, so I hesitated to send any of our men after him. But the natives are keen to find him and once they had grieved for their women, most of whom were dead, several parties of them set out to trace him. With any luck they will find him and bring him back."

"Good, good, David."

Merriman mumbled something more and then he was asleep to be roused by the shuffling of feet and muted whispers. Sleepily opening one eye, he found a deputation of seamen in front of him with the man in front, Williams, his cox'n, being nudged forward.

"Go on, tell him, he won't bite," said one.

Williams drew himself up to his full height and said, "I'm elected spokesman, sir. All the men want you to know how pleased we all are to see you getting better, sir, and they asked me to give you this."

'This' was a roughly wrapped parcel and, on opening it, Merriman found six mats, table mats, made of cunningly and neatly woven pieces of rope and canvas and coloured linen.

"The men made them for you, sir. Peters told us yours had been lost so we thought…"

"Thank you all very much, lads. I really appreciate this and…"

Matthews interrupted him by shouting, "A cheer for the Captain, lads."

Merriman was amazed at the volume of noise that erupted and he looked up to see men up the masts, on the spars and every possible vantage point from where they could see him. His officers stood in a group, grinning and smiling, and rarely had Merriman felt so moved. After leading men to possible death or injury they could still cheer him. He felt a prickling under his eyelids and waved his arm in thanks. Then the Doctor was there, ordering men to carry him down to his cabin.

"Thank you, Doctor, I felt that I might have broken down if you hadn't moved me. I had no idea that the men thought so much about me."

"Oh they do, sir, they do. I could see that it was affecting you, sir, so I had Biggins and another man carry you down. Didn't want the men seeing you shedding tears."

"Thoughtful of you, Doctor, thank you. Now leave me."

Once alone, the dam broke and he wept for Cuthbert, Weston and Hungerford but mostly at the thought of how much his men loved him.

Prisoners executed

Once the doctor announced him fit enough, Merriman was astounded by visits from all the officers from the Company ships who wished to see him and offer their congratulations and good wishes. Even Dumont the prisoner wanted to offer his congratulations. The Frenchman was no longer wearing shackles and was trusted to move as he wished, although always with two big marines guarding him. There was so much excitement and enthusiasm that Merriman insisted on inviting them all to a meeting and dinner the following evening.

At that meeting, when all of them were settled, he started the proceedings by saying, "I think that we have been here long enough, gentlemen. All ships, including the prize, are seaworthy and as for the prize I am hoping that you can each spare a few men to help my prize crew. There are only two things left to consider, one is what do we do with our captives and the other is what about Den Bosch? If the natives don't find him soon, we'll have to leave him. What do you gentlemen feel we should do with the prisoners we took? As far as I am concerned I think they should all be hanged and quickly. If we take them back to Bombay they will be hanged anyway."

There was no discussion on that matter. All agreed to have them executed the next morning. Captain Fitton said, "I think one of the sloops should leave right away and report back to the Governor, he must be desperate for news. Some of us should stay a day or two longer to see if Den Bosch is found. I think all Bombay would like to see the man who has caused us so much trouble."

All agreed on that also and Merriman called for Peters and Tompkins to serve the dinner. And a sumptuous dinner it was. Fresh roast pork bought from the natives, sweet potato and other vegetables, followed by a concoction of tropical fruits. Captain Fitton had brought over some of his own selection of wines and the evening was getting louder and louder when a loud scuffling outside the door quietened everyone.

The sentry thumped his musket on the deck and called, "Officer of the watch, sir, master at arms and prisoner, sir".

They entered. Lieutenant Shrigley, the officer of the watch, followed by the master at arms and two marines dragging their prisoner.

"What's this, Mr Shrigley, who have you got there?" demanded Merriman.

"I'm sorry to interrupt the festivities, sir, but I thought all you gentlemen would like to meet this man. The natives just brought him to us, sir. He is Den Bosch. They caught him in the jungle with some of his men. They killed the others but decided to bring him to you."

All the officers gazed with distaste on the wretched man in front of them. He was bearded and unkempt, unshaven for days and filthy dirty, covered in scratches, sores and bruises from his time in the jungle.

"Take him away and chain him up, Lieutenant, but not with the others. There we are, gentlemen, our problem is solved. I see no reason why we should not leave tomorrow after we have rewarded these people for their assistance in dealing with these cutthroats. I think we should leave them with some of the cutlasses and such that we captured, with a special gift to the chief. What do you think?"

So it was done, the seven pirates were dragged ashore and hanged from a hastily contrived gallows formed by a spar lashed between a pair of convenient palm trees in full sight of the people they had offended. Once dead, they were cut down and buried in the jungle in a place which would likely be considered haunted in future by the native people.

The prisoner Den Bosch had been thoroughly washed down by sea water and was made to watch the spectacle, standing there in his heavy chains. Merriman had a large piece of canvas spread out on the sand and had his men lay out the arms taken from the pirates. Bolts of coloured cloth from the pirates' booty were also laid out and a very special silk material was given to the chief, together with one of the French swords, one with a gold encrusted hilt. He received all this with gratitude, embracing Merriman and giving him a gift of a native dagger. Then they left, with the natives running the boats out to sea and all waving at the white men who had saved them.

Three days out, a great deal of shouting broke out and Merriman hastened up on deck to find a crowd of men and officers leaning over the foredeck rail.

"All right, all right, what's the matter? Has nobody got anything better to do?" shouted Merriman.

"It's the prisoner Den Bosch, sir. He hit a guard with his chain, not seriously, and then he jumped and scrambled onto the bowsprit, sir. He is still there, sir, won't move and curses anybody who speaks to him," reported Lieutenant Shrigley.

"All right. I'll try, Alfred, but move all those men away first."

Merriman looked over and saw the miserable man clinging to the spar with his feet dangling below him.

"Don't be a damned fool, man. Climb back here or you'll slip and drown."

Den Bosch shouted back, "What does it matter to you, Captain? They will hang me when you get back to Bombay, so what does it matter?" He threw his head back and yelled, "Damn you, damn you all," then loosened his grip and, letting out a final shriek, he fell straight down to be run over by the ship's prow.

The men all rushed to the taffrail but he had disappeared. "He's gone, sir, we can't see him."

"No, you won't. If the ship didn't hit him and kill him his chains would drag him straight down anyway." Merriman paused. "Perhaps it's better this way. He would have had a trial but he was doomed by all he did. Forget him, Alfred, and don't worry about it."

Chapter Forty

Hero's welcome

When the fleet entered Bombay harbour to the crashing of gun salutes and the cheering of the crowds of men and women on the quayside, it seemed that all the population of Bombay was there. The fast sloop sent ahead to tell the Governor to expect them had arrived but the welcome was exceptional. A large dais had been erected with an awning spread over it and everyone who was anyone seemed to be there, the women waving their parasols and the men throwing their hats in the air. Two lines of sepoy troops were between the quayside and the Governor's party but they were struggling to keep a pathway open. The shouting and cheering was deafening and Merriman and his officers were almost overwhelmed by the press of people around them.

A smart carriage took Merriman, Grahame, and Andrews to the Governor's residence where there were even more people.

"You are a hero, Captain," exclaimed the Governor, throwing his arms round him. "An absolute hero. Captain Fitton's reports which you sent in the sloop reached me and gave me all the details. He was at pains to ensure we fully understood that the success is all due to you, sir, your planning and clear thinking, and the actions of your ship. Now come with me, gentlemen."

In a daze the three of them were introduced to person after person until they could no longer keep count. Even Mr Goldberg pressed Merriman to accept their thanks. Then they were ushered into the Governor's office where long cool drinks and snacks were laid out before them. The doors were shut and all took off their coats at the Governor's suggestion and sank thankfully into comfortable chairs.

The Governor was practically bouncing with excitement, asking questions one after the other until Merriman raised his hand in protest. "Mr Duncan, sir, I am sure that Captain Fitton told you all that was needful but I must also confirm that all the Marine ships and complements did what was asked of them without fault."

"I'm sure that they did, Captain, and I would like to hear everything again tomorrow, but for today I think you would like to rest. You were wounded, I hear."

He reached into a drawer and pulled out a packet of letters, sorted through them then held two of them to his nose and said with a smile, "A lady's perfume, I think. I'm sure you want to go back to your ship to read them, Captain, but first I must tell you about the arrangements we have made for tomorrow." He presented a list of things to each of them and said, "What do you think of that? We have been very busy organising all that."

Again they were astonished at the preparations but Merriman couldn't wait to get back to the privacy of his cabin and read his letters so they soon left through the crowds back to their boat.

"My God, I've never seen anything like it before," said Grahame while Andrews shook his head in bemused silence.

A bag of post for the men had been brought out to the ship in their absence and, as soon as he could, Merriman escaped to his cabin to read his own letters. They were both dated on the cover so that he knew which was first, but he found himself pacing round the cabin, hesitating to read them, fearful of what he might find.

At last he sat, took a deep breath, and opened the first one. It was from Helen, she said she loved him and wanted him back as soon as possible, but the sad news she had to impart was that his mother had died soon after he left and his father had died some weeks later. Her father had tended them both and had told her that they had both been content at the last. The next most important news was that she was pregnant and expected the birth in only a few weeks. The letter finished with more expressions of love and longing and ended with 'Your ever-loving wife, Helen'.

Merriman sat there, savouring to himself the thought of being a father, then he reached out for the second letter, noticing only then that it was written in a different hand. He tore it open, his fingers fumbling and expecting the worst. *Has Helen died in childbirth? Is she ill? Was the child dead or not expected to survive?* His frantic thoughts were set at nought as soon as he read the first sentence. It was written by his mother's friend, Annie, and she was writing because Helen had strained her wrist and couldn't write. The most important news was that he was father of a fine healthy son and both were doing well. Helen's father, Doctor Simpson, was ecstatic at being a grandfather…

At that point, Merriman let out such a shout that the marine sentry and others rushed in to see if he was all right.

They found him leaning back in his chair, laughing out loud and pounding his hand on the desk. When he could stop laughing he waved the letter at them and said, "Gentlemen, I am a father, a boy, and all is well."

All crowded round him offering their congratulations. Word seemed to pass through the ship like lightning and soon the whole crew were cheering him again and again. He found himself on deck, surrounded by his men, all laughing and cheering.

"David, tell the purser to issue a double tot of grog to all and tell him not to object or I'll have him thrown overboard."

The backslapping excitement seemed to go on and on. Men were toasting to his health and that of his new family, with more cheering until at last he managed to escape to the quietness of the great cabin to laugh and gloat privately over his great good fortune. Now he had to go home as soon as he could, but he realised there was still a lot to be done before he could achieve that.

Chapter Forty-One

Victory. Tipu is dead. The threat in the East is over

The next day all Bombay was like one huge party as Merriman, his officers and Mr Grahame were rowed ashore to the waves and cheers of the people thronging the quayside. There was a strange canvas-shrouded item in the bottom of the boat but he soon forgot it as they all waved to the crowd. On the quayside, the canvas was whipped off to reveal a chair. Merriman's officers put him in it then the seamen lifted him up and carried him up to the Governor's residence. He was most embarrassed but soon realised that he could do nothing about it so he accepted it and was soon laughing and waving to the people. Even the sepoys lining the way were grinning all over their faces.

Finally it was over and they were in the Governor's office, relaxing over glasses of punch. Mr Duncan raised his glass.

"Gentlemen, a toast to the new father amongst us and may he and his family prosper!"

After the acclaim died away, he spoke again, "You all know that we are to have a great feast and party tonight in celebration of your exploits and victories, but we decided that the crew of your fine ship should not be forgotten. So there will be oxen roasted on big fires and plenty to eat and drink, all on the quayside. I should also tell you that Captain Fitton has offered the services of his men to get your men back to the ship in the early hours. His own people will have their own celebrations tomorrow. And now, with your permission, I should like to visit your fine ship, sir, this afternoon, with some of the senior Company Factors."

A party of them arrived on the deck of the *Lord Stevenage* later that day, in awe of the immaculate turn out of the ship and the men. Of course they all wanted drinks and, after what seemed like endless conversations and congratulations, Merriman was glad when they finally left the ship in peace. The crew had to be told of the events planned for them and Merriman called for all hands on deck. He stood at the quarter deck rail looking down on their expectant faces looking up at him.

"Men, the Governor and Authorities here have honoured you by preparing a great feast for you all tonight. You are all invited and I will let you go, but I must insist on certain things. You must all wear your best clothes and you must all behave yourselves and not let me down by bad behaviour. Remember that the town is out of bounds and if you get too drunk to know what you are doing, you will be thrown back into the boats by the crew of the Company ships and taken back to this ship. Any man who disobeys my orders will be punished. Is all that clear?"

A roar of approval rose and the men dismissed eagerly, looking forward to their party.

In the early evening, when the main heat of the day had gone, Merriman and his officers and midshipmen, wearing their best uniforms, with shoes brightly polished and their swords agleam, were taken once more to the Governor's residence. There they received the same kind of greeting as had been given when they first arrived in Bombay. The magnificent feast was served but this time Merriman was at pains to ask for advice before trying some of the dishes.

Eventually the toasts and speeches began and he wondered if it would ever end. Secretly he longed for the speeches to be over so he could take some fresh air. Most of the speeches were almost inaudible in any case as the speakers seemed mostly to be far gone in their cups. Then the Khansamah, or butler, shouted for silence for his Excellency the Governor.

Duncan rose to his feet, swaying slightly, seemed at a loss for words then remembered what he had to do. "Ladies and Gentlemen and our esteemed guests of the evening, the officers of the *Lord Stevenage* and the officers of our own Company Marine. I am not going to speak again about all that Captain Merriman and his ship have done for us, we all know that well enough, but what I am going to tell you is that I am sending a request to our Head Office in London, no dammit, a demand that they give the Captain some sort of award for his valour. I have suggested a special sword, Captain, and I am sure it will be provided in due course. No, don't thank me, Captain, it is richly deserved."

More applause came and Merriman's own officers and those of the Marine rushed to congratulate him as he sat there in a bewildered state. The noise was just beginning to die down when the Khansamah pounded on the floor with his staff and shouted, "Your Excellency, sahib, there is a messenger from General Stuart sahib waiting outside."

"Well bring him in then," said a suddenly sober Governor

All sat in silence as a weary cavalry officer, and Merriman was surprised to recognise Captain Carter, crossed to the Governor's table, saluted and said, "Dispatch from General Stuart, sir. It's all over. There has been a great battle at Seringapatam, we have won a great victory and Tipu is dead."

Silence fell for a moment and then the room erupted.

Bemusedly Merriman realised that his orders had been carried out and the threat of Tipu's navy would be over. If Napoleon and his grand army crossed Egypt he would find no fleet to help him. The *Lord Stevenage* could finally go home.

- THE END -

Author Biography
Roger Burnage (1933 to 2015)

Roger Burnage had an eventful life that ultimately led him to pursue his passion for writing. Born and raised in the village of Lymm, Warrington, Cheshire, United Kingdom, he embarked on a journey of adventure and self-discovery.

Roger's life took an intriguing turn when he served in the Royal Air Force (RAF) during his national service. He was stationed in Ceylon, which is now known as Sri Lanka, where he worked as a radio mechanic, handling large transmitters.

After his release from the RAF, Roger went on to work as a draughtsman at Vickers in Manchester. Through dedication and hard work, he eventually climbed the ranks to become a sales engineer. His job involved traveling abroad to places like Scandinavia and India, which exposed him to new cultures and experiences.

It was during this period that Roger Burnage stumbled upon the Hornblower novels by C. S.

Forester. The captivating tales of naval adventures ignited a spark of interest in the historical fiction genre within him.

Eventually, Roger settled in North Wales, where he focused on building a business and raising a family. Throughout his professional and personal life, the desire to write for himself
never waned. However, it wasn't until retirement that he finally had the time and opportunity to pursue his dream of becoming an author.

Despite facing initial challenges and enduring multiple rejections from publishers and agents, Roger persevered. He refused to give up on his writing aspirations. Even when he underwent open-heart surgery and had an operation for a brain haemorrhage, he continued to work diligently on his craft. Typing away with only two fingers for months on end, he crafted "The Merriman Chronicles."

In 2012, with the support of his youngest son, Robin, Roger self-published his debut novel, "A Certain Threat," on Amazon KDP, making it available in both paperback and Kindle formats. His determination and talent began to bear fruit, as his fan base grew, and book sales remained strong.

More information about "The Merriman Chronicles" is available online

Follow the Author on Amazon

Get notified when a new books and audiobooks are released.

Desktop, Mobile & Tablet:
Search for the author, click the author's name on any of the book pages to jump to the Amazon author page, click the follow button at the bottom.

Don't forget to leave a review or rating too!

For more background information, book details and announcements of upcoming novels, check the website at:

www.merriman-chronicles.com

You can also follow us on social media:-

https://twitter.com/Merriman1792

https://www.facebook.com/MerrimanChronicles

Printed in Great Britain
by Amazon